GREAT MYSTERIES

King Arthur

OPPOSING VIEWPOINTS®

Look for these and other exciting *Great Mysteries: Opposing Viewpoints* books:

GREAT MYSTERIES

King Arthur

OPPOSING VIEWPOINTS®

by Michael O'Neal

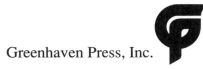

Greenhaven Press, Inc.   P.O. Box 289009, San Diego, California 92198-9009

Library of Congress Cataloging-in-Publication Data

O'Neal, Michael, 1949-
    King Arthur : opposing viewpoints / by Michael O'Neal.
        p.   cm. — (Great mysteries)
    Includes bibliographical references and index.
    Summary: Examines the conflicting evidence about the existence and historical basis of the legendary British king.
    ISBN 0-89908-095-2 : (acid free paper)
    1. Arthur, King—Juvenile literature.   2. Britons—kings and rulers—Biography—Juvenile literature.   3. Great Britain—Antiquities, Celtic—Juvenile literature.   4. Great Britain—History—To 1066—Juvenile literature.   5. Arthurian romances—Sources—Juvenile literature.   [1. Arthur, King.   2. Kings, queens, rulers, etc.   3. Great Britain—History—To 1066.]   I. Title.   II. Series: Great mysteries (Saint Paul, Minn.)
DA152.5.A7054   1992
942.01'4—dc20   92-11421

For Laurie
Who helps me perceive, understand, relish.

The snow may never slush upon the hillside,
By nine P.M. the moonlight must appear.
In short there's simply not
A more congenial spot
For happily-ever-aftering than here
In Camelot.

from the Broadway musical *Camelot*

Contents

Introduction

This book is written for the curious—those who want to explore the mysteries that are everywhere. To be human is to be constantly surrounded by wonderment. How do birds fly? Are ghosts real? Can animals and people communicate? Was King Arthur a real person or a myth? Why did Amelia Earhart disappear? Did history really happen the way we think it did? Where did the world come from? Where is it going?

Great Mysteries: Opposing Viewpoints books are intended to offer the reader an opportunity to explore some of the many mysteries that both trouble and intrigue us. For the span of each book, we want the reader to feel that he or she is a scientist investigating the extinction of the dinosaurs, an archaeologist searching for clues to the origin of the great Egyptian pyramids, a psychic detective testing the existence of ESP.

One thing all mysteries have in common is that there is no ready answer. Often there are *many* answers but none on which even the majority of authorities agrees. *Great Mysteries: Opposing Viewpoints* books introduce the intriguing views of the experts, allowing the reader to participate in their explorations, their theories, and their disagreements as they try to explain the mysteries of our world.

But most readers won't want to stop here. These *Great Mysteries: Opposing Viewpoints* aim to stimulate the reader's curiosity. Although truth is often impossible to discover, the search is fascinating. It is up to the reader to examine the evidence, to decide whether the answer is there—or to explore further.

"Penetrating so many secrets, we cease to believe in the unknowable. But there it sits nevertheless, calmly licking its chops."

H.L. Mencken, American essayist

Prologue

Ghostly Hoofbeats

At the edge of the rolling uplands, in Dorset County in southwest England, a hill stands apart from its neighbors, about five hundred feet above the surrounding farmland. The hill is largely encircled by trees, but there is a steep path leading up from the nearby village of South Cadbury. The nearly flat top consists of several acres of pastureland, but at various times in recent centuries, it has also been used for farming. On a warm summer afternoon, the verdant hill at South Cadbury near the bank of the river Cam is a picture of peace and serenity.

According to local legend, though, this hill from time to time takes on a very different character. As the evening mists settle around the shoulders of the hill and the warmth of the midsummer day gives way to the chill of darkness, there can be heard—first faintly, then more insistently—the sounds of ghostly hoofbeats on the hill. The horses, so the legend goes, are ridden by an ancient British king and his band of knights. The men in suits of armor carry lances and broadswords. Their horses are gaily decorated, and they take the steep hill almost at a canter, as if they can smell a coming battle and are impatient for it to begin. From the top, the men ride down the southwest side of the hill, water the horses at a nearby

(Opposite page) Some historians believe that this hill in South Cadbury was the site of Camelot, the home of King Arthur.

King Arthur and his valiant knights of the Round Table, from the frontpiece of *The History of Prince Arthur*, written in 1634. The legend of King Arthur has inspired artists, poets, and writers throughout history.

spring, then disappear into the mists. Morning comes, and the hill is restored to tranquillity.

Skeptics, of course, say that the legend is pure fantasy, born of the need to believe in a bygone era of heroism and chivalry. Yet for centuries, people have gazed at that silent hill and wondered what secrets lie buried beneath its calm surface, what stories the hill could tell about the people who might have lived and fought there. One who wondered was a local resident and amateur archaeologist named Mary Hatfield. On many lazy summer afternoons in the 1920s, Hatfield would walk over the hill, poking in the loose shallow soil with the pointed end of her umbrella. In this way, she found many pieces of pottery and other objects that she turned over to a local museum for examination by experts. Farmers over the years had plowed up coins and other artifacts, many dating back thousands of years. But some of Hatfield's finds were unusual and tantalizing because they were dating not to the Stone Age but to the fifth and sixth centuries.

Historians and archaeologists from all over the world came to the site and unearthed more objects from the same time period. They were excited because the objects suggested that the legend of the hoofbeats had in it a grain of truth. The objects suggested that the hill could have been the site of Camelot, the home of Arthur, that heroic warrior king, and his knights of the Round Table.

When Mary Hatfield bent down to pick up a button, a knife, or a shard of pottery, perhaps the last hand to have touched that object was the hand of King Arthur.

Was the hill beginning to give up some of its secrets?

One

The Story of King Arthur and the Knights of the Round Table

In the closing years of the twelfth century, England and France were emerging from the darkness and barbarism of the early Middle Ages. The nobility, who lived in castles and manor houses, were interested in new ideas. Their homes were becoming centers of learning and places where poets and traveling musicians and entertainers called minstrels gathered to share their stories with cultured listeners.

The owner of such a castle in twelfth-century England, welcoming a minstrel onto the estate, often knew in advance what the stories would be about. Audiences wanted tales of heroism and high adventure, but at the same time they wanted true stories about real events. Storytellers tried to please by drawing on three groups of stories. One group was referred to generally as The Matter of Rome, which also included ancient Greece. These stories featured the events before, during, and after the famous siege of Troy. Another group was called The Matter of France. These stories detailed the exploits of Charlemagne (Charles the Great), the legendary French king who lived from 742 to 814 A.D. The third group of stories, which grew in popularity during the twelfth century, was called The Matter of Britain. Throughout Europe, storytellers and their

(Opposite page) In Arthurian legend, Arthur becomes heir to the throne of Britain when he effortlessly pulls a sword from a stone.

IVRE REX BRITANNIÆ

HOW ARTHVR DREW THE SWORD

In the twelfth century, storytellers enthralled audiences with heroic tales about Rome, Greece, France, and Britain. The famous siege of Troy was a popular topic.

audiences grew increasingly fascinated with tales about King Arthur and Queen Guinevere, their magnificent castle at Camelot, Merlin the magician, Lancelot and Galahad and the other knights of the Round Table, and the ongoing search for the Holy Grail.

Audiences were hungry for these stories. The printing press had not been invented yet, so books had to be laboriously copied by hand, one by one. Even for the nobility, books were expensive—and hard to find. To learn about the outside world, these men and women relied on the rich body of oral literature that was carried to them by poets and minstrels. In the absence of reliable history books, listeners accepted the stories they heard as true.

But were they? In general, the answer is no, not entirely. By its very nature, oral literature changes over time. As storytellers traveled from town to town, they came across new versions of traditional stories, which they incorporated into their own. To make the stories interesting and exciting for their listeners, they exaggerated and embellished their tales. They transformed the characters into dashing and larger-than-life figures. Sometimes, they deliberately changed the stories in ways they knew would please their patrons and hosts. As a result, any story that circulated was likely to exist in many different versions.

To speak of *the* story of Arthur, then, is wrong, for over a period of several hundred years, Arthur appeared in many stories based on The Matter of Britain. Most of these stories were known only in parts of England and Wales. In the twelfth century, however, their popularity grew when the French writer Chrétien de Troyes published a popular written version read throughout France and the British Isles. Other French and German writers during the same period spread Arthur's fame even farther. Late in the fifteenth century, all of these oral and written versions of the tales were pulled together by the British writer Sir Thomas Malory in a book called *Morte Darthur* (The Death of Arthur). Malory took the skeleton stories about Arthur and the Round Table that had circulated for centuries and fleshed them out. He wrote the book in the squalid conditions of a London prison, but he portrayed Arthur's kingdom, the land of Camelot, with color and pageantry. Readers today picture Camelot as an enchanted place where courageous knights fight in armor and noble ladies live in turreted castles. They owe that picture to *Morte Darthur*, which five hundred years later remains the most influential version of the story of King Arthur and the one on which modern versions of the tales are most likely to be based. The following is a summary of Malory's rich and exciting tale.

Arthur's Birth

Arthur's father, Uther, the king of Britain, was at war with the rebellious Duke of Cornwall. At the same time, he was in love with the duke's wife, Ygerne. With the help of Merlin the magician, Uther

The exploits of the legendary French king Charlemagne, or Charles the Great, were often depicted in twelfth-century heroic tales.

"Whoso pulleth out this sword of this stone and anvil is rightly born king of all England."

Sir Thomas Malory, *Morte Darthur, Book I*

presented himself to Ygerne disguised as the duke. As a result of this deception, Ygerne conceived and gave birth to a son named Arthur. Merlin predicted a glorious future for Arthur and placed him under the care of Sir Ector to be raised as his foster son.

When Uther died, Arthur was not acknowledged as the rightful heir to the throne because of the circumstances of his birth. With no single king to unite the country, civil war broke out as several lesser kings fought for the throne. (Britain at this time was not a single nation but a loose collection of smaller kingdoms.) In an effort to settle the dispute, the archbishop of Canterbury invited all the British nobles to London. Ector took his son Kay and the young Arthur with him. The archbishop showed the nobles a block of stone with an iron anvil on top. A

At Lake Avalon, King Arthur receives the magical sword Excalibur from the Lady of the Lake.

sword was driven through the anvil into the stone. An inscription said that whoever withdrew the sword was the rightful heir to the throne. Many tried, including Kay, but without success. Finally, Arthur effortlessly pulled the sword from the stone and gained a kingdom.

Arthur as King

Arthur's stunning feat, however, failed to convince several of the warring nobles that he should be king. They challenged Arthur's right to the throne. But with the combined help of the sword and Merlin's power, Arthur was able to defeat them. As the years passed, he gained control over more and more of Britain, bringing peace to the land. During one campaign, he broke his sword in combat. Merlin took him to the Lake of Avalon, where the Lady of the Lake gave him Excalibur, a magnificent jeweled sword. During another campaign, he married Guinevere, the daughter of an ally.

For many years, Arthur and Guinevere enjoyed a glorious reign over a splendid court at Camelot. They passed the time in royal hunts and jousting tournaments, surrounded by the noble and courteous knights of the Round Table. The Round Table was a gift to Arthur and Guinevere at the time of their marriage. Because no one could sit at the head of a round table, it ensured that all of the knights would be equal. Each knight had his name painted on a seat, but one place, called the Siege Perilous, or Perilous Seat, was reserved for the knight who would find the Holy Grail, the mystical cup that Christ used at the Last Supper. Any other knight who sat in the seat would die.

Many of the knights had perilous adventures of their own, often to aid the victims of injustice. As a result, Arthur's realm continued to grow. It extended not only over the British Isles but over the European continent as well. The greatest threat to Arthur came from Rome. Arthur refused to pay tribute to the

"'That is the Lady of the Lake,' said Merlin, 'and within that lake is a rock, and therein is as fair a place as any on earth, and richly beseen; and this damosel will come to you anon, and then speak ye fair to her that she will give you that sword.'"

Sir Thomas Malory, *Morte Darthur, Book I*

Romantic stories about King Arthur and his queen, Guinevere, give the legend much of its fascination.

Roman emperor, and he mounted an attack against the emperor's forces. The Roman emperor sent an army into France to stop the advancing British forces. The two armies met at Troyes in France, where Arthur won a decisive victory. He now ruled over France and was declared emperor of Italy by the pope. Under Arthur's rule, Europe enjoyed a long and peaceful period.

The Quest for the Holy Grail

One night, a vision of the Holy Grail appeared at Camelot. Accompanied by loud thunder and a brilliant light, it floated into the hall where the knights were dining. After the vision passed through the hall, many of the knights vowed to go in search of the Grail. Among them were Bors, Perceval, Lancelot, his son Galahad, and Arthur's nephew

Gawain. Arthur agreed to let them go, but he was saddened. He knew that the knights would face grave dangers and that many would not survive. The Order of the Round Table and his own glorious reign were fast coming to an end.

The knights rode out, each pursuing his separate quest. They wandered about in unknown parts of Britain. They had mysterious visions and encountered strange hermits who taught them lessons about how to better their lives. They were often tempted to abandon the quest. As Arthur predicted, many failed to survive the perils they encountered and never returned to Camelot. Because of his many virtues, Lancelot was given a glimpse of the Grail in the enchanted castle of Carbonek. Later, Bors, Perceval, and Galahad arrived at Carbonek, where they were given a longer glimpse. Christ appeared to the knights and told them that the Grail would have to be taken out of Britain because of the sinfulness of the people.

Bors, Perceval, and Galahad boarded the ship that the Grail was on, bound for the Spiritual Palace in the mythical city of Sarras. There, they were permitted to see the Grail one last time. Only Galahad, the most saintly of the knights, was allowed to gaze at it at length and understand what it had to reveal. Moments later, he died, and the Grail was taken up into heaven. Bors returned to Britain, where he recounted his adventures to what was left of Arthur's court. Perceval stayed in Sarras, where he achieved fame as a noble knight and later died. Neither ever learned what Galahad really saw.

The End of Camelot

The dispersal of the knights on their quest for the Holy Grail was not the only thing that weakened the foundations of Camelot and the Order of the Round Table. Arthur was beginning to suspect something that nearly everyone else already knew—that Sir Lancelot, the bravest and the most gallant of

"So passed on all that winter with all manner of hunting and hawking, and jousts and tournaments were many, between great lords."

Sir Thomas Malory, *Morte Darthur, Book XVIII*

the knights, was in love with Queen Guinevere.

At first, their love was innocent, but soon it grew into a passionate and stormy affair. Arthur ignored what was happening because he did not want to quarrel with Lancelot. But the treachery of Guinevere and Lancelot destroyed the peace and honor Camelot represented. Out of bitterness over the death of a kinsman, one of the knights poisoned some apples that the queen served at a feast. When one of the guests died from eating an apple, the queen fell under suspicion of trying to kill Gawain, whose fondness for apples was well known. In another incident of distrust, Guinevere nearly drove Lancelot mad with her bitter jealousy after Elaine, the Fair Maid of Astolat, fell in love with him. Guinevere was abducted by Sir Mellyagraunce, who long had lusted for the queen but knew that he could

In Arthurian legend, Arthur's glorious reign is brief. The treacherous love affair between Guinevere and Lancelot (pictured here) weakens Arthur's rule over the court at Camelot.

never win her favor. Lancelot—the most skilled of the knights in the art of war—felt that he disgraced himself when he was wounded trying to rescue her. Finally, one night, several of the knights broke into a room where Lancelot and Guinevere were together. Fighting broke out, and several knights were killed. The scandal was now out in the open. Arthur had no choice but to confront Lancelot and punish the treasonous queen.

A Court Divided

The open break between Arthur and Lancelot sharply divided the court. Many knights remained loyal to Arthur, but some supported Lancelot. As the queen was about to be burned at the stake at Arthur's command, Lancelot and a party of followers rescued her and swept her away to Joyous Garde, his castle. But in the fight with Guinevere's guards, Lancelot killed Gawain's brother Gareth. Gareth's death was an accident, but because he was unarmed, his death aroused Gawain's bitter hatred toward Lancelot.

Arthur and his forces surrounded Joyous Garde, and eventually, they reclaimed Guinevere. Although Lancelot and the king both seemed ready to settle the dispute, Gawain's hatred stood in the way, forcing Lancelot and his followers to France. Arthur pursued them, leaving his illicit son Modred in charge in Britain. Modred—who for a long time had been trying to create discord in the court—took advantage of Arthur's absence. He seized the throne, telling the people that Arthur was dead. He imprisoned the queen in the Tower of London and tried to force her to marry him.

When Arthur heard the news of Modred's treachery, he and his army returned to Britain. War broke out as Arthur tried to land his ships at Dover. Gawain fell in combat, but before he died, he wrote a letter to Lancelot, forgiving him and urging him to settle his differences with the king. Arthur waited for Lancelot to return, hoping that together they

"And then [Galahad] began to tremble right hard when the deadly flesh began to behold the spiritual things. Then he held up his hands toward heaven and said: 'Lord, I thank thee, for now I see that that hath been my desire many a day.' . . . and then suddenly his soul departed to Jesu Christ."

Sir Thomas Malory, *Morte Darthur, Book XVII*

could put down the rebellion. But suspicion and distrust continued to shape the course of events. Arthur and Modred met to discuss the terms of a truce. Each feared the other, so both ordered their men to attack if anyone pulled a sword. One soldier was bitten by an adder, and when he unthinkingly drew his sword to kill it, fighting broke out. Both armies were destroyed. Although Arthur killed Modred, Modred managed before he fell to slash Arthur's head, giving him a mortal wound.

Arthur's Death and Burial

With the help of Bedivere, one of the few remaining Round Table knights, the dying Arthur made his way to a chapel near a lake. There, Arthur asked Bedivere to hurl his sword Excalibur into the water, then return and report what happened. Bedivere thought that it would be a shame to lose such a beautiful sword, so he hid it, instead. He then told Arthur that when he threw the sword, he saw only the water ruffled by the wind. Arthur knew that Bedivere was not being truthful, so he repeated his order—with the same result. Arthur grew angry, so after he ordered Bedivere for the third time to throw Excalibur into the lake, Bedivere complied. He reported to Arthur that an arm rose out of the water to catch the sword, brandished it three times, then pulled it under. Arthur knew then that Excalibur had been returned to the Lady of the Lake.

The time had come for Arthur to depart. He asked Bedivere to take him to the water's edge, where a boat appeared with women in mourning. They took Arthur aboard and bore him away to his final resting place on the mythical Isle of Avalon.

Bedivere wandered on horseback through the forest until he came to the abbey at Glastonbury, in southwest England. There, he found the archbishop of Canterbury kneeling next to a new tomb—presumably, where Arthur had been buried. Many people, however, claimed that Arthur was not dead

The mortally wounded Arthur orders Bedivere to return Excalibur to the Lady of the Lake.

When Arthur dies and his court disperses, the few remaining knights set out to fight in the Crusades.

and that, in fact, he would return to win new glory. The Latin inscription on his tomb seemed to indicate that Arthur would indeed return. It read, "Here lies Arthur, king that was, king that shall be."

Guinevere, deeply saddened by the ruin she felt she had caused, retired to a convent, where she lived the rest of her life in penance. When Lancelot returned from France, he said a final good-bye to Guinevere, then retired to Glastonbury to live as a hermit. When Guinevere died, she was taken to

Glastonbury and buried beside Arthur. In time, Lancelot died and was buried at Joyous Garde. The few remaining knights of the Round Table journeyed to the Holy Land to fight in the Crusades.

Fact or Legend?

This brief summary of *Morte Darthur* incorporates the main events of most of the Arthurian legends. But it fails to capture the ability of the story to move and excite the reader. Richard Cavendish, a scholar and critic who has written extensively about the Arthurian legends, summarizes why readers

A page from Malory's *Morte Darthur* depicts knights jousting.

during the late Middle Ages found the legends so stirring and memorable:

> Arthur and Merlin, Guinevere and Lancelot, Gawain and Galahad . . . were thought of as real people. . . . They had lived close to valour, beauty, love and luxury, but also cheek by jowl with pain, fear, sorrow and death. The tales of their adventures were exciting and enjoyable, simply as adventures, but since they were about real people they were also instructive and inspiring. They showed how men and women could best live their lives in an imperfect world.

As in Malory's time, most readers today find the tales instructive and inspiring. Unlike Malory's readers, however, most assume that The Matter of Britain is fiction, the product of the storyteller's imagination. But is it?

These stories continue to tease historians, archaeologists, and others with questions about their validity. Scholars want to know if Arthur was a real person, and they try to locate the scenes of his life, asking if Camelot really existed. They want to know if the Holy Grail existed and what form it took and whether it had spiritual powers. They continue to probe archaeological sites, trying to find Avalon, the burial place of Arthur and Guinevere.

They wonder what they would discover if they followed those ghostly horsemen down the slope of the hill at South Cadbury into the mists.

"'For Madam,' said Sir Lancelot [to Guinevere], 'I love not to be constrained to love, for love must arise of the heart and not by no constraint.'"

Sir Thomas Malory, *Morte Darthur, Book XVIII*

Two

Was King Arthur a Real Person?

(Opposite page) King Arthur as depicted in a fourteenth-century painting. The haunting mystery surrounding Arthur continues to fuel debate about his existence.

The search for the real King Arthur begins on another windswept hill somewhere in the south of England.

Preparations are underway for a mighty battle against a foe that has pillaged the British Isles for years. A number of military leaders have tried to fight off the invaders, but none have been successful. Arthur and his troops are eager to change that. They know the stakes are high. If they win, their civilization will be saved from the ravages of conquest, at least for a time. If they lose, their way of life might be swept aside forever.

More than six hundred years later, an English priest named Layamon celebrated the battle that began that day in a stirring epic poem called *Brut*. He describes Arthur and his warriors as they are about to spring into action:

Even with the words   that the king said,
He raised high his shield   before his breast,
He gripped his long spear   and set spurs to his horse.
Nearly as swiftly   as the bird flieth,
There followed the king   five and twenty thousand
Valorous men,   raging under their arms,
Held their way to the hill   with high courage.

The battle is fierce and bloody. But Arthur and his warriors fight with courage and skill. After three days of vicious combat, Arthur wins his most celebrated victory. The scene of this victory is a place called Mount Badon.

The Importance of Mount Badon

In the years around 500, the Roman Empire was losing power and becoming incapable of defending its faraway outposts. As a result, most of Europe was being overrun by fierce bands of marauders from the north. In places like France and Italy, the Goths—one of the fiercest of these tribes—met with little resistance from the people, who reacted to the invasions with either fear or indifference.

The Angles and the Saxons—two Germanic tribes who combined forces and became known as the Anglo-Saxons—met with a very different

Saxon invaders land on the shores of the British Isles. Some historians believe that the Saxons' near conquest of Britain prompted the rich body of Arthurian literature.

In addition to the threat of the marauding Anglo-Saxons, Britain was raided by the fierce, warlike Picts.

welcome when they crossed the North Sea and invaded the British Isles. There, they encountered a class of nobles who refused to let their country be overrun by barbarians. These nobles, wealthy and well-educated, saw themselves as part of the Roman Empire. They believed they represented the values of civilization and progress. With steely determination, they resisted wave after wave of Anglo-Saxon invaders, who seemed interested only in plundering the land and slaughtering the people. From time to time, the Anglo-Saxons were able to establish a foothold in some part of the country, but the Britons were able to keep them in check.

This state of affairs changed when a British chieftain named Vortigern gained power and

The British chieftain Vortigern enlists bands of Anglo-Saxons to help the Britons fight the Picts. In exchange, the Anglo-Saxons were allowed to settle in Britain.

influence. Vortigern was being harassed by another warlike tribe called the Picts. To fight them off, he hired bands of Anglo-Saxons as soldiers. As payment, Vortigern promised to allow the soldiers to settle in Britain, where they would have more room to expand than in northern Europe. In this way, the Anglo-Saxons gained a permanent place in Britain.

Warfare between the Britons and the Anglo-Saxons, however, soon broke out once again. To reduce their threat and keep them confined to the southeast part of Britain, a British leader named Ambrosius Aurelianus gathered an army and attacked the Anglo-Saxons. Although he killed the Saxon leader in battle in 488, the ferocity and strength of the invaders made it clear that they could never be driven out. This victory, however, did give hope to the Britons and showed them that they could successfully fight the Anglo-Saxons.

Defeat at Mount Badon

A few years later, Britain recorded its first major military victory. Ambrosius's second-in-command led an army of Britons against the Anglo-Saxons at a little hill called Mount Badon. There, he defeated them decisively, and Britain enjoyed a fifty-year period of peace. The architect of that victory was destined to grow into a figure of legend. His name was Arthur.

From this kernel of historical fact arose the rich, exciting, and diverse body of literature called The Matter of Britain. Almost immediately, tales were told about Arthur's heroism. These tales, with embellishment and exaggeration, were handed down from generation to generation. Soon, their larger-than-life quality made it easy for some people to conclude that they were fairy tales and that such a person never existed. In 1113, for instance, a group of priests from France was touring the county of Cornwall in southwest England. They carried with them holy relics, which they believed had healing powers. These were people who were able to believe in what they could not see. They were approached by a Cornishman with a deformed arm, who asked for their prayers. Soon, he was telling the priests stories about a legendary British hero, King Arthur, who had lived in Cornwall in ancient times, had fought valiantly against foreign invaders, and was still alive, preparing for a return to glory. The priests laughed at this tale, and when the townspeople supported the Cornishman, a street brawl broke out. Even in the twelfth century, some people doubted that Arthur ever existed.

A few years later, though, a scholarly monk named William of Malmesbury went to the abbey at Glastonbury to do research for a book he was writing about the history of England. There, he heard many of the legends that passed about among the monks. Although William did not believe many

Arthur defeats the Anglo-Saxons at the Battle of Mount Badon. After this victory, Arthur's feats of heroism were embellished and he became a legendary figure.

of the stories he heard, he did arrive at a conclusion that is shared by most historians today: Arthur was a Briton, probably of Roman ancestry, who lived in the fifth century. He led the fight against Anglo-Saxon invaders and won a stunning victory against them at a place called Mount Badon. It is ironic that Arthur is a hero to the British, most of whom are descended from the Anglo-Saxons Arthur defeated.

The Origins of The Matter of Britain

Historians generally agree that Arthur really existed, but they do not always agree on what is known about him. One of the reasons the Dark Ages—the early centuries of the Middle Ages, from about the year 476 to 1000—are "dark" is because very little written material describing the people, places, and events of that time has survived. Much of what did survive is not completely trustworthy. As a result, historians do not know very much about that era. Even most of the early evidence that Arthur actually existed is weak. It consists of brief references to Arthur, the battles he won, and some scenes of his life.

The earliest document that scholars have found that refers to Arthur by name comes from the country of Wales, in the western part of Britain. This document is a seventh-century poem called the *Gododdin*. Like most poetry from the period, the *Gododdin* is about feats of heroism in war. In one part, the poet laments a British warrior who fell in a battle in northern Britain: "He glutted black ravens on the rampart of the fort, though he was not Arthur." That is, he provided slain soldiers for the birds to feed on—though not as many as someone like Arthur would have.

Is this reference to Arthur reliable? Richard Cavendish points out that many British nobles named their sons Arthur and that Arturus was a common Roman name. So it is possible that the Welsh poet was referring to someone other than *the*

"Arthur was an authentic person . . . probably a king or a prince."

Leslie Alcock, *Arthur's Britain*

"Arthur was neither a fifth-century hero, nor associated with southern Britain. . . . He was transformed into the pseudo-historical and legendary figure who has held men's imaginations ever since."

Richard Barber, *The Figure of Arthur*

Arthur. Cavendish and historian Elizabeth Jenkins also admit the possibility that the phrase "though he was not Arthur" may have been added to the poem later. This kind of addition was not unusual in an age when scribes and others would often freely change a document to bring it up-to-date. But most historians, including Cavendish and Jenkins, agree that the line from the *Gododdin* probably refers to the legendary Arthur.

The next reference to Arthur appears in a set of documents called the Easter Annals. The Annals are part of a collection called *Historical Miscellany* housed in the British Museum. Because Easter is a feast that falls on different dates each year, churches needed to keep orderly calendars, which they then used to compute when Easter would occur in future years. This was the primary purpose of the Annals. But the Annals also became a convenient way to keep brief, year-by-year records of important events. Two notations in the Annals refer to Arthur. The first is dated 518. It reads: "Battle of Badon in which Arthur carried the cross of Our Lord Jesus Christ on his shoulders for three days and three nights and the Britons were victors." The second, dated 539, refers to Arthur's death: "The strife of Camlann in which Arthur and Modred perished."

Questions Remain

References like these seem to prove that Arthur existed and that at least some of the historical events associated with him really occurred. Archaeologist Leslie Alcock believes that these references are authentic because the Annals consistently refer to actual, historical people rather than legendary ones. But Alcock, like most scholars, hesitates to say that these references are firm proof. He raises a number of important questions about these notations in the Easter Annals.

First, it is possible that the entries in the Annals were made long after the events occurred. This

The glories of Arthur arise from his major triumph at Mount Badon. But historians disagree: Did Mount Badon really exist?

increases the chance that the references to Arthur were based on legend rather than fact. It is also possible that the specific references to Arthur were added later, as they might have been in the *Gododdin*. As new Annals were compiled, the old notations were copied into the new books, creating an opportunity for a monk or scribe to add Arthur's name to events that did take place. Further doubt about the authenticity of the Annals is cast by Saint Gildas. In 540, he wrote a book about the Saxon invasions of Britain. He mentions Mount Badon, but he never mentions Arthur. This omission weakens the authority of the Annals.

The Annals raise a second question concerning the site of Arthur's major military triumph, Mount Badon. Alcock points out that historians have proposed many possibilities for the location of Badon, but no one has offered convincing proof. Did the place really exist? Someday, perhaps a historian or archaeologist will uncover evidence to show where Arthur enjoyed his major triumph.

The Annals state that Arthur carried a cross on his shoulders for three days. Alcock points out that this statement does not seem very believable, which calls into question the accuracy of other statements. Alcock says the statement might be explained in two logical ways. One is that Arthur was carrying a relic, a small piece of something believed to be the cross, rather than the cross itself. The other is that Arthur had an image of the cross painted on his shield. The Welsh word for "shoulder" is very similar to the word for "shield," and the writer translating the entry into Latin might have simply made a mistake.

Finally, most historians believe that Arthur lived in southwest England and Wales. Some, however, present evidence that he lived in *northern* Britain. In the nineteenth century, J. S. Stuart Glennie gathered extensive evidence that Scotland, to the north, was the scene of Arthur's life. More recently, writers like Norma Goodrich have argued the case for a "northern Arthur." If they are right, this calls into question the truth of the Easter Annals and later documents that say Arthur lived in southwest Britain.

The History of the Britons

While the Easter Annals contain only brief mentions of Arthur, *The History of the Britons*, compiled in about 800 by a Welsh monk named Nennius, gives a fuller description of Arthur's activities. Most important is a list of twelve battles in which Arthur fought, ending with a reference to Badon: "The twelfth battle was on Mount Badon, in which nine hundred and sixty men fell in one day from one charge by Arthur, and no one overthrew them except himself alone. And in all the battles he stood forth as victor."

Scholars have pored over Nennius's list of battles, but the sites of only two can be located on a map with any certainty. The rest are referred to by

"The birthland of the Traditions of King Arthur was Arthurian Scotland."

J.S. Stuart Glennie, *Arthurian Localities*

"All traditions agree. His home was in the West Country. . . . The poets of the north sang about him, not because he lived there, but because . . . his northern campaigns left an undying memory."

Geoffrey Ashe, *King Arthur in Fact and Legend*

Two notations in the Easter Annals refer to Arthur. Some scholars suggest that these references prove the historical existence of Arthur.

place names for which no record exists. This by itself leads historian Richard Barber to believe that the list of battles is fictional and that Nennius's book is flimsy evidence that Arthur even existed.

This list of battles poses another problem. Scholars have suggested many possible locations for the other ten battles If even some of the possibilities are true, Arthur fought in battles hundred of miles apart all over the British Isles. In days when an army's ability to move was limited, this would have been impossible. Historian R.G. Collingwood, however, has offered an intriguing solution to this problem. He suggested that Arthur, like the Romans before him, used mounted troops rather than the slow foot soldiers typical of other British leaders of his day. This would explain not only Arthur's success but also his widespread fame, for mounted troops could have ranged far and wide. Collingwood was unable to provide clear evidence in support of this view, but it remains a tantalizing possibility.

The History of the Britons is important because it seems to confirm that a great battle was fought against the Anglo-Saxons at Mount Badon and that Arthur was the leader of the victorious British forces. At the same time, the book casts some doubt on whether Arthur was a king, as he is usually portrayed in the Arthurian legends. Nennius says, "Then Arthur fought against [the Anglo-Saxons] in those days with the kings of the Britons but he himself was leader of battles." Rather than using the Latin word *rex*, meaning "king," Nennius uses *dux*, meaning something like "duke." Later, Nennius even uses the phrase "Arthur the Soldier." This suggests that Arthur was not the king of popular imagination, reigning over a court that ruled all the British Isles. It suggests that he was a noble or a great military commander, perhaps of troops provided by several kings in the region.

The History of the Kings of Britain

The account that most strongly established Arthur as a prominent historical figure was *The History of the Kings of Britain*, written in 1135 by Geoffrey of Monmouth, a Welsh monk. As the book's title suggests, it provides a history of the earliest kings of Britain—ninety-nine in all, including King Coel, known to children from the nursery rhyme as Old King Cole.

Geoffrey devotes about one-fifth of his book to Arthur. In contrast to the piecemeal accounts of traveling storytellers, Geoffrey provides the first organized version of the story, giving it a beginning, middle, and end. Many of the elements found in later Arthurian legends, however, are missing. For example, according to Geoffrey, Arthur's court is not at Camelot but at a place called Caerleon-on-Usk, or City of Legions. But Geoffrey did contribute at least three new elements to the sketchy histories of Arthur that had circulated up to this time. He supplied Arthur's family tree, told of his association with Merlin, and described his burial at Avalon. Using the information that Geoffrey provided, later chroniclers would develop more complex stories that firmly established the reality of Arthur as a king in the popular imagination.

Arthur as King

Geoffrey's account of Arthur's ancestry begins with Constantine, the legitimate king of Britain in the fifth century. His son Constans, the rightful heir to the throne, was murdered by Vortigern, who then seized the throne, made peace with the Saxon invaders, and married the daughter of the Saxon king. Constantine had two other sons, Aurelius and Uther Pendragon, who had been taken for safety to Brittany, a region in France that was home to many Britons who had fled the Saxons. These two later returned to Britain and opposed Vortigern. Aurelius assumed the throne but was murdered by a treacherous Saxon. His successor, Uther, met a similar fate, leaving Arthur—just fifteen—as king. Geoffrey describes Arthur's reign as glorious. Arthur mounted a campaign against the Saxons and routed them at Mount Badon. He enjoyed equal success as a warrior abroad. He married a Roman woman named Ganhumara, who in the tales of later writers became Guinevere. Although Geoffrey never mentions a Round Table, he does say that Arthur was the leader of a band of knights that included Gawain, Bedivere, and Kay. Arthur's sword in Geoffrey's *History* is called Caliburn.

Geoffrey's description of the end of Arthur's reign is similar to Malory's. While Arthur is abroad, Modred revolts, plunging Britain into civil war. Arthur returns and meets Modred in battle at Camlann in 542. Geoffrey, however, does not say that Arthur dies, as the entry in the Easter Annals does. Instead, Geoffrey tells his readers that Arthur

Geoffrey of Monmouth's *History of the Kings of Britain* details the history of the early kings of Britain, including Constantine, who ruled Britain in the fifth century.

was borne away to Avalon so that his wounds could heal. He tells the same story in more detail in a later book, *Life of Merlin*:

> The Island of Apples [Avalon], which men call the Fortunate Isle, is so named because it produces all things without toil. . . . Thither, after the battle of Camlan, we brought the wounded Arthur . . . Morgen [Morgan le Fay, Arthur's half-sister] received us with suitable honors. . . . At last she said that health could return to him if he would stay with her for a long time and was willing to accept the benefits of her healing art. Rejoicing, therefore, we committed the King to her.

Clearly, Geoffrey's book was not history, as later ages would understand the term. Although it draws on factual information from earlier sources, it includes much that is fanciful and exaggerated, and it easily slides back and forth between history and fiction.

Merlin the Magician

One of the fictional elements of Geoffrey's book that continues to intrigue modern readers is Arthur's association with Merlin the magician. Although Geoffrey introduced Merlin into the Arthurian tales, most scholars agree that the character of Merlin originated elsewhere. Historian Roger Loomis argues that Geoffrey based Merlin on the character Myrddin found in Welsh legend. Folklorist Harold Massingham, however, traces Merlin back even further, claiming that he was a real king who lived in the Bronze Age.

Merlin first appears in Geoffrey's *History* as a young boy whose mother is a princess and whose father is a demon. Already a seer, the boy predicts to Vortigern that Arthur, under the name "the boar of Cornwall," will defeat the Anglo-Saxons. Geoffrey also credits Merlin with magically bringing an ancient stone monument from Ireland to Britain. The

"The *History of the Kings of Britain* . . . was one of the world's most brazen and successful frauds."

Roger Loomis, *The Development of Arthurian Romance*

"Geoffrey himself may not have made up quite as much of it as was once supposed."

Richard Cavendish, *King Arthur and the Grail*

The fanciful story of the sorceror Merlin continues to intrigue readers. According to Arthurian scholar Norris Lacy: "He is puckish and benevolent and constantly makes use of his shape-shifting powers to aid and befuddle."

monument, restored on Salisbury Plain, is today known as Stonehenge.

Merlin's association with Arthur begins before Arthur's birth. The story Geoffrey tells about Merlin's role in Arthur's birth was what Malory based his version on five centuries later. When Uther falls in love with Ygerne, the wife of a rebellious Cornish duke, Merlin appears on the scene to help him. He magically alters Uther's appearance so that he looks like the duke. Uther goes to Tintagel Castle, where the duke has left Ygerne while he is at war. Uther succeeds in his deception, and Arthur is conceived and born.

In the early years of Arthur's reign, Merlin is frequently at the center of events. Norris Lacy, a prominent Arthurian scholar and editor of *The Arthurian Encyclopedia*, describes him this way: "He is puckish and benevolent and constantly makes use of his shape-shifting powers to aid and befuddle." He serves as Arthur's wise counselor and prophet, using his magical powers to shape the course of events. He is "certainly the most colorful . . . character in Arthurian romance," according to Lacy.

By the time Geoffrey wrote *The History of the Kings of Britain*, the line between fact and fiction in the tales was almost completely gone. Geoffrey had no interest in writing an authoritative history. His service—and it was a valuable one—was in gathering together many of the ballads, legends, and tales that for centuries had floated around western Britain, especially Wales. As time went on, and as more and more copies of Geoffrey's book became available (each one laboriously copied by hand), it

Geoffrey wrote that Merlin used his magical powers to bring an ancient stone monument, Stonehenge, to Britain.

The British king Henry II encouraged the growth of Arthurian legend because it gave Britain a glorious past.

became a kind of best-seller—not only in Britain but on the European continent as well. With the encouragement of the British king Henry II and Queen Eleanor, the book and stories based on it were widely circulated. Henry and Eleanor wanted to be sure that The Matter of Britain would rival in fame The Matter of France. They also wanted to encourage the belief that Henry was descended from a noble and heroic ancestor.

Henry also wanted people throughout Europe to believe that Arthur was British rather than Welsh. It is clear, however, that many of the stories and legends that Geoffrey gathered originated in Wales rather than Cornwall, Somerset, or any of the other English districts. For example, an important tale in the early history of Arthur is a Welsh poem called

"Culhwch and Olwen." Culhwch is a young hero who is given a series of impossible tasks by Olwen's father. If Culhwch successfully completes the tasks, he will win Olwen's hand in marriage. He completes them with the aid of his cousin Arthur and many of Arthur's warriors, including Kei (Kay), Bedwyr (Bedivere), and Gwalchmei (Gawain). Incidentally, in this story, Arthur is married to Gwenhwyvaer—an early variant of the name Guinevere. Arthur is called a "sovereign prince" and has a court, but it is clear that he is not a king.

In some of the Welsh stories, particularly those recorded by the monks at the abbey at Llancarfan in Wales, Arthur is not even much of a hero. A few of the stories suggest that he may have plundered the Welsh church to supply his army. Another tale, the *Life of St. Cadoc*, portrays Arthur, who leads a small band of warriors, as quarreling with Saint Cadoc and demanding cattle as repayment for an injury. In the *Life of St. Carannog*, Arthur steals a portable altar belonging to that saint. And in the *Life of St. Padarn*, Arthur tries to rob the saint but apologizes when Saint Padarn miraculously sinks Arthur up to his neck in the earth. Clearly, Arthur was not always thought of as the hero that later generations made him out to be—at least, not in the tales recorded by these Welsh monks. Stories like these lead archaeologist Geoffrey Ashe to conclude that the real Arthur may have quarreled with the church. This would explain why no complete and reliable history of Arthur was written: the people who would have written such a history—the monks who lived in abbeys and monasteries—did not like or admire him.

Conclusions

Faced with these conflicting traditions and accounts, what conclusions have modern historians drawn about Arthur? In general, they agree that a hero named Arthur did exist, although no evidence suggests that he was ever acknowledged as king of

Britain. He was born in about 470 into a Christian family that still sympathized with Rome and its way of life, even though the British Isles were coming out of Roman rule. He probably started his career as a local chief or noble, but as his reputation for valor spread, he gathered around himself an army of knights who fought where their services were needed. In due course, Arthur led a major expedition against the Anglo-Saxons, and his victory over them early in the sixth century assured his fame. On at least one occasion, Arthur had to fight his own countrymen in a civil war, and he finally died in that

The legend of Arthur flourished because it promoted romance, chivalry, and noble ideals during a dark and savage time.

The legend of Arthur spread as far as the Middle East. This may explain why Arthur is here depicted riding a camel.

war at the hand of Modred. This is the foundation of fact on which the structure of the Arthurian tales was later built. But no one knows how much, if any, of the other details of the early Arthurian legends are true.

The Matter of Britain was quickly becoming an important part of the literature and history of western Europe. Because of the close cultural ties between Britain and France, the legends of Arthur freely moved across the English Channel. The stories then spread across the continent, eventually reaching as far as the Middle East. These tales became enormously popular, particularly among the nobility and upper classes, who responded to the gallantry of Arthur and his knights.

But the legends were still relatively young. New generations of poets would find in the Arthurian tales fertile ground for their imagination, and the stories would continue to grow and develop.

Three

The Order of the Round Table

To celebrate Pentecost, which commemorates the appearance of the Holy Spirit to the apostles, Arthur and his knights sat down to a grand feast. Typically, they waited for an unusual event to occur before they dined. On this occasion, Gawain looked through the window and saw three men approaching the castle in the company of a dwarf.

The three men, wearing elegant robes, entered the hall and approached the king. The tallest of the three greeted Arthur, then asked the king to grant him three gifts. Struck by the noble bearing of the man, Arthur granted him his request.

To everyone's surprise, the man asked only for food and drink—and for permission to request his other two gifts one year later. Arthur readily agreed.

A year later, the knights once again sat down to their Pentecost feast, once again they waited for something unusual to occur, and once again they were not disappointed. An unknown noblewoman entered the hall, knelt before the king, and told her story. Her sister was being held captive by a cruel knight, and she beseeched the king, "who is said to command the flower of chivalry," to dispatch one of his knights to her rescue. Gawain pointed out to the assembled company that the knight the noble-

(Opposite page) King Arthur presides over the knights of the Round Table. The vast body of Arthurian literature includes many versions of the origin and significance of the Round Table.

Sir Gareth defeats the fearsome Red Knight, earning a place at the Round Table. The theme of valorous knights on dangerous missions was prominent in many of the Arthurian legends.

woman described was the Red Knight of the Red Rocks, and that he had the strength of seven men.

The lady was reluctant to give the name of her sister or tell where she lived. For this reason, Arthur refused to offer assistance. At this point, the tall man to whom Arthur had granted three requests stepped forward to claim the remaining two. He asked to be allowed to aid the lady and her sister, and he asked to be accompanied by Lancelot. If he proved worthy in his quest, he wanted to be sworn into the Order of the Round Table by Lancelot, "who is peerless among all knights."

Arthur granted the mysterious man's request, and he and Lancelot set out on their quest. Lancelot seemed willing to knight the man but refused to do so until the man revealed his identity. Finally, the man confessed that he was Sir Gareth of Orkney, the brother of Sir Gawain, one of the prominent knights of the Round Table. Gareth wanted to be knighted but not on the strength of his relationship to Gawain. He wanted to earn a place at the Round Table by showing strength and bravery in coming to the aid of others.

Membership in the Order of the Round Table

In time, Gareth encountered the Red Knight and met him in armed combat. He was severely wounded but recovered and eventually defeated the Red Knight. In the meantime, Arthur learned of Gareth's identity and welcomed him to Camelot and the Round Table. A warm welcome was extended, too, to the sister, Lady Lyoness, of "peerless beauty and grace," who accepted Gareth's hand in marriage.

The story of Gareth illustrates the central role that the Round Table and membership in the Order of the Round Table began to play in the Arthurian tales. Sir Gareth, like many of his fellow knights, was willing to go to any length to earn the right to enjoy the fellowship of Arthur's knights. The story told about him is typical: over and over, mysterious strangers appear at court, distressed people come to ask for help, knights set out on dangerous missions and rescue women they love, and identities are eventually revealed. But it was not until after Geoffrey's *History* was published in 1135 that the Round Table became an important part of the legends. By the time Malory wrote *Morte Darthur* in the fifteenth century, the adventures of the knights of the Round Table had fully captured the imagination of readers. New stories focused on the exploits of Gareth and Gawain, of Galahad and Lancelot—solitary heroes facing danger alone.

The Origins of the Round Table

The earliest legends of Arthur told of a dark and savage time in the history of Britain. People lived perilous and uncertain lives in small communities. In exchange for their allegiance, they were given protection by a noble or king. Warfare was commonplace, and the threat of invasion by brutal pirates and plunderers was ever-present. It was a grim life, a time when brute strength and physical courage were all that ensured survival.

In 1155, however, the French poet Robert Wace imagined Arthur's world differently. His poem *Roman de Brut* (Story of Brutus), which he based on Geoffrey's *History*, was dedicated to the British queen Eleanor. Like any author trying to please a patron, Wace wanted his poem to find favor with the queen. By birth, Eleanor was French, and she was generally thought of as highly educated and cultivated. Wace wrote the poem in French, and more important, he changed the tone and atmosphere of the stories. He left out many of the brutal and violent passages in Geoffrey's version. He also added a great deal of picturesque detail, enlivening the portrait of Arthur's court with color and pageantry. But Wace's most important contribution was the Round Table. Wace did not *invent* the Round Table; it was already part of the

A knight is initiated into the Order of the Round Table. Typical of Arthurian tales, this knight is depicted as a bold adventurer.

"This Round Table was ordained of Arthur, that when his fair fellowship sat to meat, their chairs should be high alike, their service equal and none before or after his comrade."

Robert Wace, *Brut*

"The Table of Jesus Christ . . . was the table that sustained bodies and souls with food from heaven. . . . In the likeness and in remembrance of it . . . was the table of the Holy Grail . . . in the time of Joseph of Arimathea, when Christianity was first brought to this earth."

"The Quest for the Holy Grail," Vulgate Cycle

oral tradition, although its origins remain uncertain. But *Roman de Brut* is the earliest known written version of the Arthurian tales to mention this key element of the story.

According to Wace, Arthur had recruited so many valorous knights that disputes would arise about seating arrangements in the king's hall. Because a rectangular table has a head and a foot, there is a sense that those seated at it have been ranked in order of importance. A carpenter from Cornwall, according to Wace, suggested a solution to the problem. He made a huge round table so that no knight would be seated "higher" or "lower" than any other.

This version of the origin of the Round Table appeared in England at the end of the twelfth century with the publication of Layamon's *Brut*. In his poem, Layamon tried to preserve the dark, gloomy, untamed atmosphere of the Dark Ages. If in Wace's poem Arthur's knights are sometimes rivals, in Layamon's they are true combatants. One night, a brawl erupts. Arthur appears and halts the fighting, but only after much bloodshed. He restores order in a way that leaves no room for question: "Sit ye, sit ye quickly, each man on his life! And whoso will not that do, he shall be put to death." He punishes the knight who started the brawl by condemning him and all of his male relations to death; all his female relations were to have their noses cut off.

Once again, the solution to the problem comes from a Cornish carpenter, who offers to make for the king a table:

I will work thee a board exceeding fair, that thereat may sit sixteen hundred or more, all turn about so that none be outside. And when thou wilt ride, with thee thou mayst carry it and set it where thou wilt, after thy will; and then thou needst never fear, to the world's end, that ever any moody knight at thy board may make fight, for there shall the high be even with the low.

The French poet Robert De Boron, writing in about 1200, links the origin of the Round Table to the story of the Holy Grail. The Holy Grail is the cup that Christ used at the Last Supper, which early church tradition says took place at a round table. According to De Boron, the first keeper of the Holy Grail was Joseph of Arimathea, the biblical character who received permission from Pontius Pilate to take Christ's body off the cross and bury it. Joseph brought the Grail to Britain in the year 63. His goal was to establish Christianity in the British Isles. With his party of followers, he set forth from the Holy Land, bearing with him the Holy Grail. On

King Arthur's Round Table depicted in a fourteenth-century painting. According to Robert Wace, a carpenter from Cornwall proposed this table in which "there shall the high be even with the low."

Robert De Boron linked the legend of the Holy Grail—the cup from which Christ drank at the Last Supper—to the origin of the Round Table.

the journey, Joseph set up a table as a memorial to the Last Supper, called the Grail Table. One seat at Joseph's Grail Table was to be kept empty to represent the seat occupied by Judas before he betrayed Christ.

De Boron tells his readers that the Grail Table provided the model for the Round Table. In his version, however, the Round Table was made not for Arthur but for Uther Pendragon. After Uther's death, the table passed to Guinevere's father. When Guinevere married Arthur, the table went with her as her dowry. Merlin chose the knights who would sit at the Round Table and predicted that like Christ's apostles they would live in harmony. The Perilous Seat was reserved for the knight who proved himself worthy enough to find the Holy Grail.

What Does the Round Table Mean?

In less than a century, from Wace to De Boron, the meaning and importance of the Round Table had changed. In Wace's poem, the table is simply furniture that offers a handy solution to the problem of quarrels among the knights. In De Boron's tale, it gained a much richer significance. Richard Cavendish, whose book *King Arthur and the Grail* thoroughly examines the Arthurian legends, describes that significance in this way: "[The Round Table] is an exalted order of knighthood with a Christian mission. Through its link with the table of the Last Supper, it is a symbol of the fellowship of Christ and his disciples, an image of the ideal society of heaven. Its roundness is now interpreted as an emblem of the whole world."

Earlier Arthurian tales had been dominated by the king himself. His heroic exploits were captivating in an age when the courage and bravery of one leader was enough to hold a fragile community together. After the Round Table became part of the tales, the focus shifted. Now the emphasis was on the Order of the Round Table. The Round Table became a symbol of an ideal community in which all the members are equal and all contribute to the welfare of the group.

The word *chivalry* is often used to refer to the ideals that the Round Table represents. Literally, the word means "men-at-arms mounted on horses." When the noblewoman who appears at Arthur's court says that he commands "the flower of chivalry," she means that he commands the best, most skilled knights. But when applied to Arthur's knights, the word means much more. Chivalry is an ideal code of conduct. A chivalrous knight is high-minded and honorable. His bravery in battle is taken for granted. He gives unquestioning loyalty not only to his king but to his comrades as well. He treats others, especially women, with the utmost courtesy. And he uses his skill at arms to help those who most need his help.

To offer that help is not merely the knight's duty. It is his greatest wish—as it was for Sir Gareth. The highest achievement a knight can attain is to follow the code of chivalry as one of King Arthur's knights. To sit at the Round Table is as close as a man can come to achieving the ideal of earthly and spiritual perfection.

In Arthurian legend, the highest achievement a knight could attain was to follow the code of chivalry.

Four

The Fall of the Order of the Round Table

(Opposite page) Lancelot comes out of Guinevere's room and is confronted by a band of knights. The love affair between Lancelot and Guinevere is a harbinger of the fall of the Order of the Round Table.

The legends of King Arthur are vague about time. They take place in a faraway world that is not governed by the clock or the calendar. It is clear, though, that Arthur presides over the Order of the Round Table for many years.

But the Round Table is not destined to last forever. Layamon imagines the collapse of the Order of the Round Table in an incident recorded only in his poem *Brut*. Layamon says that Arthur had a dream in which Modred and Guinevere betray him. In the dream, Arthur is sitting on the roof of the hall. Modred begins to chop down the supporting pillars with an ax, while Guinevere tries to pull down the roof. Arthur falls to the ground, breaking his arm, but he manages to cut off Modred's head. He then cuts the queen in pieces and hurls her into a black pit.

Arthur's dream suggests that the Order of the Round Table has a sinister side. For later writers, an important part of the drama of the Arthurian tales would be the fall of Arthur's realm when the ideals of the Round Table are betrayed. Although Guinevere and Modred participate in that betrayal, it is Lancelot, Arthur's friend and the bravest knight of the Round Table, who sows the seeds of the

Guinevere dubs Lancelot her sworn protector. The French poet Chrétien de Troyes was the first to weave their illicit love affair into Arthurian legend.

destruction of Camelot and King Arthur's glorious reign.

At the end of the twelfth century, the French poet Chrétien de Troyes wrote five long poems about the knights of the Round Table, each telling the tales of a single character. Chrétien's tales are graceful and elegant, but they are also important because they are the first version of the Arthurian legends to mention Camelot, Sir Lancelot, and the illicit love affair between Lancelot and Queen Guinevere. That love affair—a betrayal of Lancelot's friend and Guinevere's husband—was destined to undermine the Order of the Round Table.

Chrétien's treatment of the Lancelot story is a good example of how the tastes of an audience can influence an author's approach. Chrétien lived in Troyes, in eastern France, at the court of the count of Champagne. His patroness there was Countess Marie, the daughter of the British queen Eleanor by her first marriage to King Louis VII of France. Marie, like her mother, was interested in romantic tales, particularly those in the tradition of courtly love. This tradition emphasized the love affairs of elegant and fashionable people, particularly those who served at the courts of the nobility. Usually, these love affairs thrived outside the bounds of marriage. In an age when most marriages were arranged by parents without regard to the feelings of the couple to be married, the elaborate conventions

An illustration of Lancelot and Guinevere reveals the aura of chivalric romance that was incorporated into many Arthurian tales.

of courtly love—the hidden messages, the midnight meetings, the violent emotions—provided a romantic escape. For Marie and her companions, stories of courtly love had an aura of sophistication and excitement. The love these stories depicted was forbidden, so all the more appealing. Chrétien's tales helped spread the conventions of the courtly love tradition throughout France and England. The forbidden love of Lancelot and Guinevere added a dash of romance to tales that had traditionally stressed war and feats of arms.

Chrétien made Lancelot the most noble champion of the Round Table: "No knight ever sat in a saddle, who was the equal of this man," he wrote. There is no evidence, however, that Lancelot was a real person. Roger Loomis, in *The Development of Arthurian Romance*, argues that Lancelot's character probably came from Welsh legend. A pagan Irish god named Lugh Lamhfada developed into a Welsh warrior named Lluch Llauynnauc, who was the model for Lancelot's character. Like Lancelot, Lluch was famous both for his mastery of the arts of war and for his handsomeness.

Lancelot's Betrayal

Chrétien's story of Lancelot's betrayal begins on Ascension Day. A knight named Mellyagraunce, also called Meleagant, who is not a member of the Order of the Round Table, arrives at Camelot to announce that he is holding many of the knights and ladies of Arthur's court captive. Included among the captives is Guinevere.

By this time, Lancelot is already in love with the queen, so he gladly assumes the task of rescuing her. On his journey to a land called Gorre, where the queen is being held, Lancelot undergoes a number of tests of his valor. To enter the kingdom, for example, he has to crawl over a bridge that is a long, sharp sword. In spite of his painful injuries, he reaches the castle and fights Meleagant in single combat, inspired by the sight of Guinevere watching from a tower.

Neither knight is able to gain the upper hand, so they agree to a truce and plan to meet a year later to settle their dispute. In the meantime, Guinevere treats Lancelot coldly, upset that he did not come to her rescue sooner. But soon, she is no longer angry and falls ill with grief over the way she has treated Lancelot. Lancelot, thinking she is dead, tries to kill himself but is stopped just in time. The two agree to meet that night at Guinevere's window. The window is barred, but Lancelot finds a way in. That night, they are together for the first time.

Chrétien's story does not tell how Lancelot and Guinevere's betrayal affects the king. In *Morte*

Queen Guinevere as depicted in most legends— elegant, fashionable, and sophisticated.

Darthur, Malory would show how the passion of Lancelot and Guinevere undermined King Arthur's realm.

"The Tale of Sir Lancelot and Queen Guinevere"

When Malory wrote about Lancelot and Guinevere, he did not use Chrétien as his source. He wanted to treat the story more seriously than Chrétien had, so he relied on two other sources, both by writers unknown today. One source, written early in the thirteenth century, was called *Perlesvaus*, and it dealt mainly with the Grail quest. The other, more important source is today called the *Prose Lancelot*. Written sometime between 1215 and 1230, it was part of a larger group of Arthurian tales scholars call the Vulgate Cycle. (*Vulgate* refers to any commonly read or accepted book. Until Malory, the Vulgate Cycle, a group of five tales, was the most complete and widely read account of The Matter of Britain.) In both of these sources, the quality of the writing is unsteady, and many plot incidents are repetitive or unconnected. But in these accounts, the story of Lancelot and Guinevere is transformed into tragedy and one of the world's great love stories emerges. Later, in London's Newgate Prison, Malory further refined the story. He wrote "The Tale of Sir Lancelot and Queen Guinevere."

In Malory's version, Lancelot's passion for the queen plays a key role in the fall of the Round Table and the death of Arthur. During Lancelot's quest for the Holy Grail, he had vowed to give up Guinevere, an act of virtue that earned him a glimpse of the Grail. When he returns to Arthur's court, however, he finds that his love for her is as strong as ever. He is unable to remain true to his vow, and their affair resumes. An atmosphere of suspicion and betrayal begins to hang over Camelot.

For a long time, Arthur remains blind to their affair. He refuses to believe Agravain, one of the few knights who dislikes Lancelot, when he tries to

"*Lancelot* . . . seems to glorify the adulterous passion of Lancelot for Guinevere."

Roger Loomis, *The Development of Arthurian Romance*

"[Malory] makes it overwhelmingly clear that it was the love of Lancelot and Guinevere which wrecked the society of the Round Table."

Elizabeth Jenkins, *The Mystery of King Arthur*

destroy Lancelot's reputation by telling Arthur about the affair. Eventually, Arthur accepts evidence from another source. Lost in a forest with a number of his knights, he is welcomed at a castle that turns out to be the fortress of his half-sister, the enchantress Morgan le Fay. She, too, hates Lancelot—and Guinevere as well. She takes Arthur to a room where she had held Lancelot prisoner and where he had painted pictures with captions on the walls that leave no doubt about his relationship with the queen. Morgan confirms what the pictures show and persuades Arthur to punish the guilty pair. He returns to Camelot with that intention but soon wonders if Morgan has told him the truth. He takes no immediate action, but uneasiness grows in the court.

Suspicion infects even the queen. When Lancelot is away from court on a knightly mission, Guinevere grows jealous, believing he is having an affair with another woman. In reality, Lancelot is at Astolat, where he is recovering from injuries he received in a tournament. Nursing him is a beautiful young woman named Elaine, who falls in love with him. When Lancelot tells her his heart belongs to someone else, she pines away and dies. A letter pinned to her clothes proves Lancelot's innocence, and the queen is mortified by her hasty judgment.

Suspicion Grows

In the meantime, Guinevere herself falls under suspicion. She is seated at the table with several of the knights when a poisoned fruit intended for Gawain is delivered to her. Innocently, she offers it to another knight, who bites into it and falls dead. No motive is ever offered, but everyone, even Arthur, believes the queen is guilty. The dead knight's brother demands justice. The only way the queen can clear her name is if a champion steps forward to defeat the brother in combat. No one agrees to fight on the queen's behalf.

Lancelot, though, learns what has happened.

The enchantress Morgan le Fay, Arthur's half-sister, convinces the king to punish the guilty Lancelot and Guinevere.

Even though he thinks Guinevere is guilty, he resolves to fight for her honor. On the appointed day, he secretly rides to Camelot, enters the field against the outraged brother of the dead knight, and wounds him. The brother gratefully accepts Lancelot's offer to spare his life if he withdraws his accusation against Guinevere. Arthur comes forward to welcome Lancelot home, glad that his wife's innocence has been proved.

Lancelot's last chance to fight on the queen's behalf ends in near disaster. On a beautiful day in May, the queen, with a small party of knights and ladies, goes out into the fields around Camelot to pick herbs and flowers. The evil knight Mellyagraunce, who has lusted for the queen,

Lancelot bids adieu to the beautiful maiden Elaine, who nursed him to health after he received injuries in a tournament. A jealous Guinevere, however, suspected the two were having an affair.

The common medieval theme of tragic, forbidden love is apparent in this portrait of Lancelot and Guinevere.

appears with 160 armed men. He seizes the queen and her party and carries them off to his castle, but Guinevere manages to send a message—not to her husband but to Lancelot. Lancelot is in pursuit when his horse is hit by arrows from the evil knight's archers. He then has to make his way to the castle in a horse-drawn cart.

The appearance of Lancelot strikes fear into Mellyagraunce, who backs down from a fight with him. Lancelot and Guinevere spend the night together in her room. The next day, when Mellyagraunce finds marks of Lancelot's blood on the queen's bed, he publicly claims that one of the queen's wounded knights must have slept with her. Lancelot, to defend the queen's honor, challenges Mellyagraunce to combat in Arthur's court. When Lancelot slays him, everyone believes that Mellyagraunce had slandered the queen. "And the

Sir Lancelot in his castle, Joyous Garde. Arthur lays siege to Joyous Garde in one of his final battles.

King and Queen made more of Sir Lancelot du Lake and more was he cherished than he was aforetime," wrote Malory. Lancelot does not dispute the lie.

But finally, a trap is set that forces Arthur to admit the treachery of his queen and her lover. The vicious Modred and his brother Agravain burst into Guinevere's room and find the lovers in bed. Lancelot fights his way out, and accompanied by a party of followers, he escapes. Arthur receives the news with a sick heart. With sorrow, he orders the execution of his wife. As Guinevere is led to the place of execution, Lancelot and his followers hide in the forest. They rush at the soldiers guarding the queen, and a fierce fight breaks out. In the confusion, Lancelot accidently kills Gawain's brother Gareth, who is one of the guards. Lancelot's party seizes the queen and carries her off to Joyous Garde, Lancelot's castle.

With reluctance and sadness, Arthur lays siege to Joyous Garde. He loves both Lancelot and Guinevere and would like to be reconciled with them, but events are out of his control. One factor is Gawain's powerful rage over Lancelot's murder of his unarmed brother Gareth. Gawain challenges Lancelot to single combat but is bested. Lancelot and his followers flee across the English Channel into France. Once again, Arthur pursues them, and in his absence, a civil war erupts that leads to Arthur's death.

Guinevere expresses an understanding of the terrible consequences of her betrayal. Near the end of *Morte Darthur*, after Lancelot returns from France, she bids him good-bye and resolves to end her life in penance: "Through this same man and me hath all this war been wrought, and the death of the most noblest knights of the world; for through our love that we have loved together is my most noble lord slain. . . . And yet I trust, through God's grace and through His passion of His wounds wide that after my death I may have a sight of the blessed face of Christ Jesu."

The Quest for Ideals

The story of Lancelot and Guinevere as Malory saw it is not simply a romantic love story in the courtly love tradition, as it was for Chrétien. In *Morte Darthur*, Lancelot is a tragic figure, torn between his love for Arthur and his passion for Guinevere. That passion has serious consequences. Because Lancelot does not renounce his illicit love,

"The knight [Bedivere] cast a pitiful moan
Where he stood, sore and weak
And said: 'Lord, whither are ye bound?
Alas, whither will ye from me go?'
The king spake with a sorry sound:
'I will wend a little time
Into the Vale of Aveloun,
Awhile to heal me of my wound.'"

Morte Arthur, by unknown 14th-century English poet

"Then Sir Bedivere cried and said: 'Ah my lord Arthur, what shall become of me, now ye go from me and leave me here alone among mine enemies?' 'Comfort thyself,' said the King, 'and do as well as thou mayst, for in me is no trust for to trust in. For I must into the vale of Avilion to heal me of my grievous wound.'"

Sir Thomas Malory, *Morte Darthur, Book XXI*

When Lancelot murders Gareth, Sir Gawain (pictured here) develops a powerful hatred for Lancelot. This rage fuels the irreconcilable division at Camelot.

he is denied a complete vision of the Grail and an understanding of the Grail's meaning. More important, his passion sets in motion events that eventually destroy the Order of the Round Table and undermines the reason and goodwill that the Round Table represents. A common thread that unites the stories of the heroes of the Round Table is the temptation each feels to stray from following the path of an ideal life. When the other knights are faced with the allure of comfort and ease, they find a way to resist and remain true to the heroic ideals of the Round Table. Lancelot, however, succumbs to those temptations, destroying Camelot and the Order of the Round Table when he does. He gives up the quest for honor and holiness, betrays his king, and harms the people he loves most.

To the modern reader, the ideals of chivalry that

the Arthurian tales portray may seem far removed from present-day life. Modern literature probes the minds and hearts of characters who are fully human, with many frailties. Perhaps, however, the Arthurian tales have survived for hundreds of years and continue to be told in books, movies, and on the stage because the ideals of nobility, loyalty, courage, and grace are sought by people living in all ages.

Nowhere are those ideals—and the eternal effort to achieve them—more clearly shown than in the quest for the Holy Grail.

Colorful tales of jousting knights continue to intrigue modern readers.

Five

The Quest for the Holy Grail

For many years, the Siege Perilous was empty, waiting for the knight who was worthy enough to occupy it. One morning, Arthur, Guinevere, and the knights were assembling at the Round Table when they noticed a number of fresh inscriptions in gold paint around the empty seat. One said, "He ought to sit here." Another predicted that the seat would soon be filled.

That evening, as the knights gathered for dinner, a squire appeared in the hall and amazed the knights by saying that a block of red marble was floating down the river. All ran out to see it. Thrust into the marble was a beautiful jeweled sword with an inscription that said, "Never shall man take me hence but only he by whose side I ought to hang and he shall be the best knight of the world." Everyone assumed the sword belonged to Lancelot, but Lancelot knew that it did not. He predicted that the person who could pull the sword from the marble would fill the Siege Perilous and lead the quest for the Holy Grail.

Arthur asked Gawain to try to withdraw the sword. Gawain doubted that he was "the best knight of the world," but he tried, without success. Then Perceval tried, but he, too, was unsuccessful. No

(Opposite page) A fifteenth-century woodcut depicts the empty Siege Perilous—the seat reserved for the person destined to lead the knights on the search for the Holy Grail.

The knights of the Round Table receive a benediction before departing on their quest for the Holy Grail.

other knight was willing to try, and so they returned to the Round Table.

Shortly after the knights were seated, an ancient holy man entered the hall, accompanied by a young knight clad in red armor. The old man predicted that the young knight "shall accomplish the greatest undertaking" of Arthur's reign. The old man led the knight to the Siege Perilous and removed from it a silk cloth that Arthur had placed over it. All were amazed to see a fresh inscription that said, "This is the seat of Sir Galahad the high prince." The young knight sat in the seat without harm. All the knights knew that the one destined to lead them on their quest for the Holy Grail had arrived.

The Mystery of the Holy Grail

The Holy Grail remains the most perplexing but at the same time most intriguing part of the Arthurian legends. The different versions of the Grail story fail to provide answers to the most basic questions: What is the Grail? What does it look like? Where can the Grail be found? What is the purpose of the quest for the Holy Grail? As Roger Loomis says in *The Development of Arthurian Romance*, "The authors of the Grail texts seem to delight in contradicting each other on the most important points."

These authors agree, however, on one point. In each of their tales, the search for the Holy Grail is the central goal of the Order of the Round Table. The knights undergo extraordinary hardships to find it and understand its meaning for themselves and for the Order.

The Book of Perceval or the Story of the Grail

Although Celtic literature in the sixth and seventh centuries contains isolated references to a life-giving vessel called a *criol*, the first complete story of the Grail dates from about 1180. The author was Chrétien de Troyes, whose *Le roman de Perceval ou le conte du Graal* (The Book of Perceval or the Story of the Grail) is viewed by modern readers as the original story. Chrétien wrote the poem for a nobleman, Count Philip of Flanders, drawing on a book he said Philip had given him. If this is true, then at least one version of the story existed before Chrétien's. Chrétien died before completing the poem, leaving that task to three different writers. One claimed that he adapted his part of the story from an ancient Welsh text. If true, this would mean that at least two versions existed before Chrétien's. Neither of these sources has ever been found, so it remains unclear how much of the story Chrétien made up and how much he found in earlier books.

The central character in *The Story of the Grail* is Perceval, a clumsy and rustic young man who has been brought up by his mother in nearly complete ignorance of the world. He does not even know his name. One day, when he is still little more than a child, he encounters a band of Arthur's knights riding through the forest. Immediately, he decides that knighthood must be the road to manhood. He

"It seems clear that . . . the Grail is a Christian object."

Richard Cavendish, *King Arthur and the Grail*

"A constant feature in the Celtic legends is the quest for a magic vessel."

Elizabeth Jenkins, *The Mystery of King Arthur*

appears before Arthur and asks to be knighted, but Arthur refuses, believing that Perceval is not ready to assume the responsibilities of knighthood.

Perceval, always impetuous, rides off to prove himself, but he is distracted by a series of adventures, including a love affair with a beautiful young woman named Blancheflor. In time, he comes to a castle whose owner, Gornemant, teaches the would-be knight the principles of chivalry. Additionally, he cautions Perceval to curb his impulsiveness and not say whatever comes into his head—a troublesome habit Perceval has. Under Gornemant's guidance, Perceval develops into a skillful fighter, enabling him in later years to survive many adventures and defeat many foes.

On his journey home, Perceval comes to a river where two men are in a boat, and one of them is fishing. The fisherman offers Perceval shelter for the night in his nearby castle. Perceval accepts, but when he arrives at the castle, he discovers that his host, the fisherman, has mysteriously arrived before him. And he learns that his host is crippled. Then, something astonishing happens. A young man comes into the hall bearing a white lance. From the tip of the lance a drop of red blood runs down onto the man's hand. Two more men enter with candelabra, followed by a richly dressed, beautiful damsel. She carries a magnificent golden cup—the Grail—studded with jewels and surrounded by a brilliant light. The procession leaves the hall, but later, as each course of a sumptuous dinner is served, the Grail by itself passes before Perceval and his host.

The Fisher King

Perceval burns with curiosity, wanting to know what these mysterious events mean. He remembers the teachings of Gornemant, though, and remains silent. His curiosity grows the next morning when he awakes to find that his host and all of the guests have disappeared. Perceval then leaves the castle. As he is making his way through the forest, he finds a young girl, his cousin, who answers some of his questions. She tells him he spent the night in the castle of the Fisher King. The Fisher King is crippled and in intense pain because of wounds received in battle. To Perceval's dismay, she also tells him that his failure to ask the king why the lance bled or where the Grail procession was going will bring misery to the king, his people, and himself. Later, at Arthur's court, the story told by Perceval's cousin is confirmed by an ugly maiden, the Loathly Damsel, who scolds Perceval for missing the chance to restore the king to health and save the land from desolation.

Sir Perceval holds the Holy Grail. The quest for the Grail is a central tenet of the Order of the Round Table.

Perceval is humiliated and vows to find the Grail and ask the needed questions. While on his search, he encounters a hermit who provides more answers. Perceval's troubles, he says, stem from the grief he caused his mother when he abruptly left home to become a knight, and from his neglecting to return to her. According to the hermit, Perceval's insensitivity to his widowed mother was a sin, and this sin left him unable to know when to speak and when to remain silent. The hermit also reveals more about the Grail Castle. Living there, too, is the Fisher King's father, who is served Communion wafers from the Grail and who eats nothing else. This man, the king's father, is also Perceval's uncle. Since Perceval's own father is dead and the Fisher King has no children, Perceval is heir to the throne as well as to the Grail Castle and its mysteries. As though a spell has been broken, Perceval knows his name.

In his study *King Arthur and the Grail*, Richard Cavendish offers his view of what Chrétien's story means: "Its central theme is the hero's progress towards an ideal integrity as the best knight in the world. . . . [Perceval] learns the code of chivalry with its emphasis on duty to others. He is gradually turning into a civilized human being instead of a bumpkin." In other words, in his quest for the Grail, Perceval learns who he is and how to be a Christian knight.

Unanswered Questions

Chrétien died before completing the poem, so he left behind many unanswered questions about the Grail. He never states exactly what the Grail *is* or why it is a "holy thing." Nor does he explain why the lance bleeds or what the connection between the lance and the Grail is. And there are other questions: Why would asking the right questions heal the Fisher King—and failure to ask them lead to suffering? Who is the Fisher King? Who is the

Loathly Damsel and how does she know of Perceval's visit to the Grail Castle?

Literary historians like Cavendish and Loomis seek answers to these questions in the pagan Celtic stories they believe Chrétien used as a source. These stories share common themes: A hero loses his way, but a host invites him to a mysterious place, arriving there before him. The hero encounters magical life-giving vessels, usually borne by a beautiful maiden. The hero is supposed to ask a certain question that will heal the keeper of the vessel, restore the land to plenty, and reveal the hero as the rightful heir to the kingdom. If the hero fails to ask the right questions, the kingdom will be left with a ruler who is old and feeble, like the Fisher King's father, or lacking an heir, like the childless Fisher King. The Loathly Damsel foreshadows the horrible outcome if the hero fails in his quest.

Parzival

Another famous version of Perceval's adventure was written in Germany by a Bavarian knight named Wolfram von Eschenbach. He wrote a long and beautiful poem called *Parzival* between about 1200 and 1210. The enormous popularity of *Parzival* in the nineteenth century led the German composer Richard Wagner to use it in 1882 as the basis for a famous opera called *Parsifal*.

It is easy to assume that Wolfram based his poem on Chrétien's. Both feature the same hero, and most of the basic elements of the story—the Fisher King and the Grail Castle, for example—are found in both. Wolfram, however, said that he did not think very highly of Chrétien's poem, and he made a number of important changes.

For one thing, he changed the character of Perceval. Chrétien makes him clumsy and simpleminded to stress how the quest for the Grail civilizes him. Wolfram gives his hero far more dignity and pride, and the story emphasizes instead his need to acquire Christian humility and sympathy. During his quest, Chrétien's Perceval simply drifts away from God and the duties of a Christian knight. Parzival, on the other hand, is a rebel who openly spurns God. He believes the curses the Loathly Damsel hurls at him for failing to ask the right questions are unjust and undeserved.

Wolfram also transforms the question test. In *The Story of the Grail*, Perceval fails the question test out of ignorance and self-doubt; he lacks the

The story of Sir Perceval was popular in Germany, as this German manuscript illustration suggests. Here, Perceval—or Parzival as he is called in the German tale—prepares to depart on his quest for the Grail.

judgment to know when to speak and when to be quiet. Parzival fails for a very different reason: he lacks sympathy for others. But he, too, learns his lesson from a hermit. Not knowing Parzival's identity, the hermit tells the story of a visitor to the Grail Castle and remarks: "He must atone for that sin, that he failed to ask about his host's anguish, which was so keen that no greater was ever known." Parzival now knows what he must do to be a true knight. He returns to the Grail Castle and asks the right question: "Mine uncle, what is it afflicts thee?" Suddenly, the Fisher King, who in this version of the story is Perceval's uncle, is "whole and sound." Parzival has been successful in his quest. He has found not only the Grail but also the true path to Christian knighthood.

Finally, Wolfram makes important changes to the Grail, which is usually pictured as a vessel—a cup, chalice, or bowl. In Chrétien's poem, the Grail is used to carry the Communion wafer to the Fisher King's father. It therefore is a source of spiritual life. But Wolfram sees the Grail not as a vessel but as a stone. It is a talisman with magical powers. It is set before the king and magically provides everyone in the hall with whatever food and drink they want. Roger Loomis thinks that Wolfram took the idea of the stone from an ancient story about Alexander the Great, in which a small stone is used to teach Alexander humility, which is the same lesson Parzival learns. Richard Cavendish offers a different explanation. For him, the stone comes from alchemy —the medieval "science" based on the philosopher's stone, a mysterious substance that cures disease, turns the old young, turns base metals into gold, and gives the holder physical and spiritual life.

The Grail's Path to Britain

The early stories of Perceval and his vision of the Grail are a blend of Christian and pagan ideas. Perceval is trying to learn the duties of a Christian

"The word Grail is derived from the Latin word *gradalis*, signifying a gradual or step-by-step descent . . . to the mysterious 'red substance' of Alchemy . . . which induced the power of clairvoyant vision."

Walter Stein, "Merlin"

"It seems a reasonable conclusion that Irish *criol* . . . [meaning "bag," "basket," or "box"] . . . is the source of the French *graal*."

Arthur Brown, *The Origin of the Grail Legend*

knight. The Grail, though, has mystical powers, and its roots go back to pagan folklore. For Malory, writing more than two centuries later, the Grail was almost strictly a Christian symbol. This change was due primarily to a prose tale called *Joseph d'Arimathea*, written late in the twelfth century by Robert De Boron, a French writer about whom little is known. Most readers agree that *Joseph* is not very well written. It remains important, though, because it offers a clear explanation of what the Grail is and how it arrived in Britain. Today, many people continue to believe the story.

Joseph of Arimathea

For De Boron, as for Chrétien, the Grail is a vessel. It is the actual cup that Christ used to celebrate the first Mass at the Last Supper. The cup was given to Pontius Pilate, who, in turn, gave it to Joseph of Arimathea. Joseph was an admirer of Christ and asked Pilate for permission to bury Christ after the crucifixion. As Joseph was preparing the body for burial, it began to bleed. Joseph collected the blood in the cup, which he then hid.

Joseph, as an early Christian, was later imprisoned. While he was in prison, Christ appeared to him with the Grail. He told Joseph that only three men would ever guard the Grail. He also gave Joseph the secret of the Grail—sacred words with mysterious power that have never been revealed. During his years in prison, Joseph drew all the nourishment he needed from the Grail.

After his release from prison, Joseph and a band of Christian converts left the Holy Land, determined to settle elsewhere, taking the Grail with them. One member of the party was Joseph's sister, who along the way married Bron, known as the Rich Fisher. Bron took the Grail to a land in "the far West"— certainly Britain—and became its first keeper.

According to De Boron, Joseph was left behind, never completing the journey to Britain. In the

The Grail was a source of healing, inspiration, and vision. Some say that Joseph of Arimathea, pictured here, knew the secret of the Grail.

Vulgate Cycle, however, the story of Joseph ends differently. Joseph brings the Grail to Britain himself. Along with four thousand followers, he establishes Christianity in the British Isles upon his arrival in A.D. 63. As a result of these stories, the Grail became firmly established as a Christian relic that offers to its seekers the eternal life of Christianity.

Galahad and the Vision of the Grail

In the poems written by Chrétien and Wolfram, the central figure in the quest for the Holy Grail is Perceval. Malory, however, follows the Vulgate Cycle, which assigns the central role to Sir Galahad. Although Lancelot does not know it, Galahad is his son. One night, Elaine of Carbonek dupes Lancelot into believing she is Guinevere. Soon afterward, Galahad is born and is sent away to be raised by a group of nuns living in an abbey.

One night, a gentlewoman appears at Arthur's court and summons Lancelot to the abbey. Lancelot complies, and while he is there a noble-looking youth—Galahad—is presented to him to be knighted. Lancelot knights him, still not knowing that the youth is his son or even that he has a son. Only later, when an old man brings Galahad to Arthur's court, does Lancelot learn who Galahad is.

When Galahad takes his place in the Siege Perilous, all the knights are filled with anticipation. Now that the Round Table is complete, the quest for the Holy Grail can begin. Malory's version of the quest for the Grail emphasizes each knight's personal quest for spiritual purity. The Grail is a religious symbol, so only knights who are pure can see it. Many of the knights who seek the Grail perish in the attempt because they are unable to resist the temptations that lure them from the quest. Others

In his search for the Grail, Galahad receives a vision from an angel. His purity of body and soul enable him to obtain the Grail.

simply give up because the quest is too arduous. Only Lancelot, Bors, and Galahad are granted visions of the Grail. Lancelot, who had vowed to give up Guinevere, is rewarded with a partial vision of the Grail. Similarly, Bors is allowed only to glimpse the Grail because he felt guilty after his one encounter with a woman. Galahad, who is descended from Joseph of Arimathea, is the purest and most saintly of the knights of the Round Table. He battles his way through a horrifying wasteland, at one point accidentally coming to blows with Lancelot. He perseveres in his quest and is rewarded with a full vision of the Grail. He immediately dies, and the Grail is taken up into heaven.

In the end, Malory's Grail remains an object of mystery. Searching for it is a way to overcome obstacles and resist temptations. It is the way to holiness. Galahad has to find his way through a world of desolation, relying only on spiritual strength and on faith that the Grail exists. When he finds it, though, and understands its mysteries, he is no longer fit to live in the world. Galahad's vision of the Holy Grail gives him eternal life. But each reader has to decide what Galahad actually saw, for Malory, like writers before and after him, remains silent on this matter.

According to Malory, Galahad's vision of the Holy Grail gives him eternal life.

The Mystic Tradition

The Grail has a mysterious hold on the imagination. It appears in different places. It changes its form. It is bathed in radiant light. And it rarely relinquishes its secrets. It is not surprising, then, that almost from the beginning there grew up around the Grail explanations of its meaning that stressed its connection with secret societies and mystical wisdom.

Some historians and folklorists, for example, have suggested that the Grail stories were written in secret opposition to the teachings of the Catholic church. In *The Grail Castle and Its Mysteries*,

An angel leads knights on their quest for the Grail. According to Malory, a knight's search for the Grail was a way to overcome obstacles and resist temptation.

historian Leonardo Olschki says the stories were written as a kind of code used to spread religious heresy, any teaching the church believes is false. During the Middle Ages, the church was active in fighting sects that promoted a variety of opposing beliefs. One of these heresies was Gnosticism, the belief that all matter is evil and that spiritual salvation comes only through secret wisdom, not through the use of crosses, altars, churches, and other signs of the Christian church. Gnostics were attracted to pagan forms of worship, like the Grail procession, and they used stories about the Grail to spread their beliefs among followers.

Adherents of this mystical view of the Grail are particularly interested in Wolfram's *Parzival*, primarily for three reasons. First, the Grail in *Parzival* is a stone rather than a relic of Christ. The

Grail's power comes from magic rather than from the teachings of Christianity. Second, the poem says the stone's history was written down by a Middle Eastern sorcerer, further emphasizing the Grail's mystical properties. Finally, the Grail keepers in *Parzival* are Knights Templars, a secret, mystical knighthood—a kind of priesthood—that for centuries passed on a tradition of secret wisdom. Perceval would become the new Grail keeper only after passing the ritual tests that enable him to become a Knight Templar.

Conflicting Claims

Most modern readers reject the belief that the Grail stories hold meaning only for those who believe in a tradition of secret wisdom that has been entrusted only to members of secret sects. For most readers, the Grail simply represents an ideal that people seek, often at great risk. Rarely are ideals fully achieved, but the process of searching for them is valuable in itself. But most readers continue to be perplexed by the many questions surrounding the stories of the Grail. Part of the problem is that there is little tangible evidence to support the many conflicting claims that are made. Most scholars say they have no artifacts to show that the Grail or Camelot really existed.

Some archaeologists and historians disagree. They say that there is physical evidence, and some even claim to have found it.

"The grail, borne ahead of the procession, was worked with fine gold, and there were in the grail many precious stones, the finest and most costly in the world."

Chrétien de Troyes

"[Many brave knights] live from a stone of purest kind. . . . The stone is also called the Grail."

Wolfram von Eschenbach, *Parzival, Book IX*

Six

The Search for Arthur

If King Arthur, Guinevere, and the knights of the Round Table existed, surely they left behind some physical evidence of their presence. For centuries, historians and archaeologists have searched for that evidence, each dreaming of the day he or she would find, perhaps in the ruins of a castle, an object inscribed with a name or an ancient manuscript that would prove that some part of the stories really happened.

No such conclusive find has ever been made. The history of Arthur in archaeology, however, includes some findings at three different sites that have intrigued generations of scholars.

Tintagel Castle: The Place of Arthur's Birth?

Geoffrey of Monmouth identifies Tintagel Castle as the place of Arthur's birth. If he made this up, he was inspired, for a more suitable place for the birth of a legendary hero could hardly be imagined. The castle is located in southwest England, overlooking the widest part of the Bristol Channel. It stands atop a rocky headland. Waves crash against the cliffs below. Visitors to Tintagel feel its atmosphere of romance and adventure.

Today, all that remains of Tintagel are ruins.

(Opposite page) In the twentieth century, the work of archaelogists and historians has brought fresh insight to the King Arthur story. Some believe that Glastonbury Abbey, pictured here, is the burial place of Arthur and Guinevere.

Tintagel, located in Cornwall, is the site of archaeological investigation by Arthurian enthusiasts. Some say that Arthur was born here.

Until fairly recently, it was believed that Tintagel could not have been Arthur's birthplace for the simple reason that the castle, which belonged to an earl, was not built until about 1141—almost six hundred years too late. In the 1920s, however, the archaeologist Ralegh Radford undertook an excavation of Tintagel. He made no claim to finding proof that it was Arthur's birthplace, but he did discover that the castle was formerly a monastery probably built during Arthur's lifetime. The artifacts he found suggest strongly that Tintagel was a center of worship and learning during the Dark Ages. If Arthur lived in the region, he very well could have been a visitor to Tintagel.

Fragments of pottery, which became known among archaeologists as Tintagel ware, were Radford's most important discovery. Again, none of this pottery can be linked directly to Arthur, but it can be dated to Arthur's time. The pottery was not made locally but was imported from areas around the Mediterranean Sea. It probably was used to hold luxury goods like wine and oil. This shows that the occupants of Tintagel were wealthy and important. For Radford, Tintagel ware proves at least that the castle *could* have been home to a prominent chieftain or noble like Arthur.

Similar excavations elsewhere in Britain continued into the 1950s. Archaeologists discovered several hill forts that date from Arthur's time. These forts were not towered castles but were more like large fortified hills with earthwork walls, ramparts, and buildings used for various purposes. One of these finds, called Dinas Emrys, may have belonged to Ambrosius, who led the fight against the Anglo-Saxons before Arthur.

Cadbury Castle

The site that has attracted the most attention has been the hill fort called Cadbury Castle, near the village of South Cadbury and the river Cam. Ever since Chrétien de Troyes made the first reference to "Camelot"—perhaps a shortened form of Camulodunum, the Roman name for the city of Colchester—Cadbury Castle has been the leading candidate for the location of Arthur's court.

The first antiquarian to record a connection between Camelot and Cadbury was John Leland. Leland was the chief historian of King Henry VII of England. In 1542, Leland described what he saw at Cadbury:

> At the very south end of the church of South Cadbury stands Camelot, sometime a famous town or castle, upon a very tor or hill, wonderfully strengthened of nature. In the upper part of the coppe of the hill be 4 ditches or trenches, and a bulky wall of earth between every one of them. . . . Much gold, silver, and

"With every justification, we can think of Arthur and his troops feasting and carousing . . . in a hall similar to that at Cadbury."

Leslie Alcock, "*By South Cadbury is that Camelot . . .*"

"The enthusiastic description of the discoveries made by recent excavations [at Cadbury] as "Arthurian" are [not] warranted."

Richard Barber, *The Figure of Arthur*

copper of the Roman coins have been found there in plowing. . . . The people can tell nothing there but that they have heard say that Arthur much resorted to Camelot.

Later writers confirmed that by Leland's time, the area around Cadbury had strong associations with King Arthur. Another antiquarian, William Stukeley, visited "Camalet Castle" in 1723 and wrote:

> Camalet is a noted place. It is a noble fortification of the Romans, placed on the north end of a ridge of hills. . . . There is a higher angle of ground within, ditched about, where they say was king Arthur's palace: it was probably the *praetorium* [meeting hall], and might be king Arthur's too, who lived in this place: the country people refer all stories to him.

As the largest of the hill forts that has been found, Cadbury seems an appropriate headquarters for someone of Arthur's stature.

Excavations at Cadbury

Only in the twentieth century did serious work by archaeologists begin at Cadbury. The pottery that Mary Hatfield found by poking the ground with her umbrella turned out to be Tintagel ware. This meant that the hill fort had been in use during the time Arthur lived and revealed that the owner was a person of wealth and importance. Radford was the archaeologist who examined Hatfield's finds, and he concluded: "The small collection indicates an occupation during the fifth, sixth, or early seventh century and provides an interesting confirmation of the traditional identification of the site as the Camelot of Arthurian legends."

Beginning in 1966, Leslie Alcock, a prominent Arthurian archaeologist, began a four-year excavation of the Cadbury site. There was so much public interest in the excavation that parts of it were filmed and shown on British television. Alcock's excavation produced several exciting finds. One was a gate tower, the only such tower that has been found in hill forts. Another was a large hall, one of only three that are known to modern archaeologists in Britain. The third was a set of large defensive ramparts that encircle the fort. The shape of the hilltop would normally have required a much smaller fort to defend it. The fifth-century commander, however, decided to enclose a much larger area—eighteen acres—suggesting that the fort held a large army of perhaps as many as one thousand troops. Alcock does not argue that the commander was Arthur, but he concludes that the characteristics of Cadbury Castle are fully consistent with what is known about Arthur.

Not everyone agrees. Historian Richard Barber's book *The Figure of Arthur* is a skeptical overview of all the evidence concerning the historical Arthur. Barber believes that Arthur, if he existed at all, was no more than a "lesser figure" who lived in the north of Britain. He focuses on the detail from Nennius, who described Arthur as a "leader in battles" rather than a ruler. Barber concludes that the large fortress at Cadbury more likely belonged to Constantine, the early British king who had territory in the area, or even Vortigern. The Cadbury excavations fail to convince Barber that Arthur was anyone other than a "pseudo-historical and legendary figure who has held men's imaginations." In other words they fail to prove the existence of Arthur.

Glastonbury: The Isle of Avalon?

The third promising Arthurian site is the abbey at Glastonbury. Visitors to Glastonbury say that the place has a spellbinding attraction. Something about it draws thousands of visitors each year, some of them looking for enlightenment or heightened spiritual awareness. Others are simply curious, wondering if it is possible that Glastonbury Abbey is the burial place of Arthur and Guinevere—and if the

"The place which is now called Glaston was in ancient times called the Isle of Avalon. . . . Morgan carried [Arthur] away after the battle of Camlann to the island that is now called Glaston."

Gerald de Barri, 1193

"We must therefore dismiss Arthur . . . from any proven historical connection with Glastonbury."

Reginal F. Treharne, *The Glastonbury Legends*

abbey holds the key to the location of the Holy Grail.

The core of the abbey's appeal is the Glastonbury Legend. According to the legend, Christianity was brought to Britain in the year 63 by Joseph of Arimathea, at the request of the apostle Philip. With his followers Joseph came, bearing the Holy Grail, the sacred cup used by Christ at the Last Supper and in which Joseph had collected Christ's blood after the crucifixion. After landing in Britain, Joseph made his way to Glastonbury Tor, the cone-shaped hill that overlooks the abbey. When he arrived, he stopped to pray. He stuck his staff into the ground, and it immediately took root and budded. Today, the Glastonbury Thorn—presumed to be a later cutting from the original staff—continues to flower. Joseph declared that the site would be a place of worship, and the church he founded at the foot of the tor was the first church to be built in Britain. It became a shrine until it was destroyed by fire in 1184, although the abbey was

Glastonbury Abbey with the tor beyond. The man-made tor is associated with the Isle of Avalon. Indeed, in Arthur's time the area was a marshland and the tor rose above the surrounding water like an island.

later rebuilt. Somewhere near the foot of the tor, Joseph buried the Holy Grail for safekeeping. Although the Chalice Well, with its mysterious red water, marks the place of the burial, the Grail has never been found.

The Glastonbury Legend also says that the burial ground in the abbey is where Arthur and Guinevere are buried and that Glastonbury is the Isle of Avalon where Arthur was taken after his final battle. Today, Glastonbury is landlocked but until it was drained in the Middle Ages, the area was marshland, and the tor rose above the surrounding water like an island.

According to Arthurian legend, the dying king was borne across the water to the mystical Isle of Avalon.

The first known excavation at Glastonbury was made in the belief that the site is Avalon and in an effort to find Arthur's tomb. Sometime in 1190 or 1191, the monks at Glastonbury Abbey claimed success. The historian Gerald of Wales was present at the "discovery" of Arthur's tomb and later described what he saw:

> Arthur the famous British king is still remembered. . . . His body . . . was found in recent times at Glastonbury between two stone pyramids standing in the burial ground. It was deep in the earth, enclosed in a hollow oak, and the discovery was accompanied by wonderful and almost miraculous signs. . . . A leaden cross was found laid under a stone. . . . We saw this, and traced the inscription which was not showing, but turned in towards the stone: "Here lies buried the famous king Arthurus with Wennevereia his second wife in the isle of Avallonia.". . . What is now called Glastonbury was in former times called the Isle of Avalon, for it is almost an island.

Gerald provides additional details. For example, he claims that a lock of golden hair discovered in the tomb mysteriously disintegrated when one of the monks touched it. Fanciful details such as this might lead to the conclusion that Gerald was deceived and that the discovery was a hoax.

Ralegh Radford, however, is not so sure. In the 1950s and 1960s, Radford confirmed at least some of the details of the story. He found the pillars—the "two stone pyramids"—and established that the ground between them had been dug out. He also concluded that the area at the bottom of the hole had at one time been used as a grave.

The Leaden Cross

One detail, however, did not fit. That was the leaden cross. The cross is now lost but drawings of it survive. The lettering on the cross suggests that the monks' story is a fraud, for its style dates from about the tenth century—far too late for Arthur, who died in the sixth century.

Radford has offered a theory that solves this problem. He points out that it was common practice for burial grounds in abbeys to be layered. Space was at a premium, so when the area was filled, a deep layer of earth would be piled on and a new layer of graves started. Radford suggests that Arthur was, in fact, buried at the site. Later, in the tenth century, the monks inscribed the cross as a marker for the grave, then added a seven-foot layer of earth. When the twelfth-century monks dug for Arthur's grave, they dug through the first layer, found the cross, then dug through the second layer to find the tomb. Commenting on Radford's conclusions, archaeologist Geoffrey Ashe writes: "[The monks]

A small sign marks the alleged site of Arthur's and Guinevere's double tomb.

must have done what they said, and found the bones of a man who had been identified as Arthur much earlier. . . . There was no reason to think that he was anyone else."

Radford's conclusions have not gone unchallenged. Both Reginald Treharne, in his book *The Glastonbury Legends*, and Richard Barber, in *The Figure of Arthur*, dispute the belief that Arthur's tomb was discovered in the twelfth century. Both believe that the discovery was a hoax, part of an ingenious fund-raising scheme. In 1184, a disastrous fire destroyed much of the abbey. Then in 1189, the abbey's chief patron, Henry II, died. His successor, Richard I, showed no interest in providing money for restoration of the abbey. The monks were desperate, until they devised the plan to find the tomb of King Arthur. The publicity would attract both patrons and funds.

The discovery of Arthur's tomb would also please the British monarch. By the time of Henry II and Richard I, England was unified under the authority of a strong central government. The English kings wanted to keep it that way. Welsh tradition and folklore, however, continued to foster the belief that Arthur—a Welsh hero, to them—was alive and would some day rise up to lead Wales back to greatness. Of course, the kings of England dismissed this tradition. They did, however, worry about a false Arthur who might convince enough people that he really was Arthur to cause turmoil. Proof that Arthur was dead would end the threat of rebellion in Wales. The Glastonbury monks, in sore need of money from the king, seemed to have found that welcome proof.

Glastonbury and the Holy Grail

The monks at Glastonbury never referred to the Grail. They did say that Joseph arrived at Glastonbury with two silver cruets, or small bottles, one containing Christ's blood, the other containing his sweat. The cruets were buried with Joseph, they said, but no one knew the location of Joseph's tomb.

Nevertheless, a tradition emerged claiming that the Grail was somewhere on the grounds of Glastonbury Abbey. A few years after the supposed discovery of Arthur's tomb, a story about the quest for the Holy Grail called *Perlesvaus* appeared. The unknown author of the poem claimed that he had based his poem on a book found in the Glastonbury Abbey. No such book has been found, but the story forged a permanent link between the Grail and Glastonbury. In the nineteenth century, the story of the Chalice Well also gained wide acceptance.

According to Welsh tradition, Arthur was to one day return and lead Wales to greatness. Fearful of rebellion in Wales, Richard I tried to foster the belief that Arthur was dead.

Some people say that the Chalice Well with its mysterious red water marks the spot where Joseph buried the Grail.

Joseph, so the story goes, wanted to protect the Holy Grail, so he buried it somewhere near the foot of the tor, and there a spring emerged. Sometimes, the water that flows from the spring has a mysterious reddish tint—the color of the sacred blood the Grail once held. Although the Grail has never been found, believers say that the Chalice Well marks the spot where Joseph buried it.

The mysteries of Glastonbury have given rise to several intriguing theories about the place, theories that suggest answers about the Grail. One theory is explained by Karen Maltwood in *A Guide to Glastonbury's Temple of the Stars* and by Mary Caine in *The Glastonbury Zodiac*. According to these authors, close examination of aerial photographs taken over Glastonbury confirms that the area forms a giant zodiac—the map of the heavens used in astrology to show the influence of the stars and planets in human affairs. They believe this zodiac, whose parts are marked off by roads, rivers, and so forth, forms a kind of map that when rightly interpreted will lead one day to the location of the Grail. A competing theory is offered by archaeologist Geoffrey Ashe in two books, *King Arthur's Avalon* and *Avalonian Quest*. Ashe claims to have discovered several mazes that are formed by the natural and artificial features around the abbey and the tor. Each of these mazes has a definite design, and Ashe suggests the possibility that at the end of one of the maze's twists and turns, someone will discover the Holy Grail. So far, neither of these theories has led to any discovery.

Hitler and the Grail

The story of the quest for the Holy Grail has itself taken some bizarre twists and turns. The German dictator Adolf Hitler believed in the Grail, and he believed that the one who possessed it would rule the world. Before World War II, Hitler formed the SS, an elite, secret Nazi organization, and ordered it to find the Grail. Heinrich Himmler, the director of the SS, in turn, formed the Black Order, an inner circle of Nazis who accepted the challenge. According to author David Wilson, the Black Order was negotiating with someone in England who claimed to know where the Grail was. The war ended, however, and nothing came of this unknown person's claim. Yet the very existence of a secret government organization trying to find the Grail keeps alive questions that have been asked for centuries: Was there really a Grail? Where is it now?

"The coffin and its contents . . . were produced by the monks in order to raise the money for the rebuilding of the Abbey."

Richard Barber, *The Figure of Arthur*, on the 1191 discovery of Arthur's tomb

"The background was not the Abbey's need for money."

Geoffrey Ashe, *King Arthur in Fact and Legend*

Epilogue

"Arthur, King That Was, King That Shall Be"

(Opposite page) The legend of King Arthur embodies the notion of a faraway, magical era—an age of mystery, heroism, and noble ideals. Even in the twentieth century, the mystique of King Arthur continues to cast its spell.

Is King Arthur alive?

Reason says no. The man who led the British forces to a triumphant victory over the Anglo-Saxons in the sixth century was mortal. The Easter Annals give the date of his death.

Reason does not always prevail, however. People have an unexplained need to believe in the unexplainable. Every June, thousands of people converge on Glastonbury. Some seek a vision of Arthur; others look for spiritual enlightenment. They walk in solemn procession, devoutly believing against all reason that they can take part in the special magic of the place and its mystical power to heal and inspire.

As long as people have the power of imagination, as long as they can be inspired to heroism and to search for their personal grail, Arthur and the ideals he and the Order of the Round Table defended will live on.

Glossary

Note that the spellings of proper names are likely to vary from text to text. No standardized system of spelling existed until modern times, and writers, who worked from a variety of sources, chose the spelling they preferred.

Agravain   Modred's brother; one of the few knights who disliked Lancelot and tried to convince Arthur of the affair between Lancelot and Guinevere.

Ambrosius Aurelianus   king of Britain before Uther, his brother; leader of British forces against Anglo-Saxon invaders before Arthur.

Anglo-Saxon   refers to the two Germanic tribes, the Angles and the Saxons, that had merged by the time they overran Britain in the fifth and sixth centuries.

Avalon   the island where Arthur was taken after he fell in battle at the hand of Modred, either for burial or to recover from his injuries; presumed to be present-day Glastonbury.

Badon   the site of the battle where Arthur defeated the Anglo-Saxons early in the sixth century; although the site of the battle has not been identified with certainty, this event is presumed to have actually taken place.

Bedivere   a knight of the Round Table; remembered primarily for having to throw away Arthur's sword at his request.

Bors   a knight of the Round Table; he goes on the quest for the Grail with Galahad and Perceval and supports Lancelot after his split with Arthur.

Cadbury Castle   a hill fort near the village of South Cadbury in southwest England; thought to be the site of Camelot.

Caerleon-on-Usk   the site of Camelot according to Geoffrey of Monmouth; *Caerleon* means "city of legions."

Camelot   the legendary site of King Arthur's court; first mentioned by the French poet Chrétien de Troyes.

Camlann   the site of Arthur's final battle which occurred in 539, according to the Easter Annals.

Carbonek   an enchanted castle where Lancelot was given a glimpse of the Grail; in some versions, the place where Galahad was born.

Celtic   refers to any of the original inhabitants of the British Isles; also refers to the family of languages including Irish, Welsh, Cornish, and Breton.

Chrétien de Troyes   a major French poet who lived at the court of the count of Champagne in eastern France; first writer to mention Camelot, Lancelot, and the love affair between Lancelot and Guinevere; between 1160 and 1180, he wrote five Arthurian tales, including *Lancelot* and *The Book of Perceval or the Story of the Grail*, which was unfinished at his death.

De Boron, Robert   late twelfth-century French poet whose *Joseph d'Arimathea* is the earliest surviving story of the Grail's early history; he is important in establishing the tradition that Joseph brought the Grail to Britain.

Ector   Arthur's foster father.

Elaine   the Fair Maid of Astolat who falls in love with Lancelot and dies after he tells her that he cannot return her love; also Elaine of Carbonek, Galahad's mother.

Excalibur   Arthur's beautiful sword, given to him by the Lady of the Lake and returned to her by Bedivere just before Arthur dies.

Fisher King   Perceval's host at the Grail Castle; he appears as an old, maimed, or crippled king and is the guardian of the Grail.

Galahad   the holiest of the knights of the Round Table; son of Lancelot and Elaine of Carbonek and descended from Joseph of Arimathea; he is the only knight to be granted a full vision of the Grail.

Gareth   a knight of the Round Table and Gawain's brother; he is killed by Lancelot during Lancelot's rescue of Guinevere.

Gawain   a prominent knight of the Round Table; he initiates the Grail quest and becomes Lancelot's enemy after the death of his brother Gareth.

Geoffrey of Monmouth   early twelfth-century Welsh historian; his *The History of the Kings of Britain*, the first full and comprehensive written account of Arthur's life that has survived, was for centuries accepted as an authentic history of Britain, even though it contains much that is fiction.

Gerald of Wales   historian who described the "discovery" of Arthur's tomb at Glastonbury in 1190.

Gildas   British monk whose history of Britain, written in about 540, is important for mentioning the battle of Mount Badon and for *not* mentioning Arthur.

Glastonbury   location of the abbey where Arthur's tomb was reputed to have been found; also the presumed site of Avalon.

Gododdin   seventh-century Welsh poem that contains the earliest known reference to Arthur.

Gornemant   a hermit who instructs Perceval in the principles of knighthood and chivalry.

Guinevere   Arthur's queen and Lancelot's lover; she entered a convent after Arthur's death and was presumably buried with him at Glastonbury.

Joseph of Arimathea   presumed founder of Christianity in Britain who supposedly brought the Grail with him from the Holy Land.

Joyous Garde   Lancelot's castle.

Kay   son of Ector and one of the knights of the Round Table.

Lancelot   Often considered the most gallant and heroic knight of the Round Table; he was denied a full vision of the Grail because of his illicit love affair with Guinevere, which eventually divided Arthur's court and led to the fall of the Round Table.

Layamon   English priest who wrote the first surviving Arthurian tale (*Brut*) in English late in the twelfth century.

Malory, Sir Thomas   British writer, born 1410, died 1471; while in Newgate prison, he wrote the most famous and widely read story of Arthur, called *Morte Darthur* by his printer, published in 1485.

Mellyagraunce (also Meleagant)   an evil nobleman who abducts Guinevere and takes her to his castle, where Lancelot rescues her.

Merlin   the magician who aids Uther in his deception of Ygerne and who becomes Arthur's chief adviser early in his reign; he first appears as part of the Arthurian legends in Geoffrey of Monmouth's history.

Modred (also Mordred and Medraut)   Arthur's nephew (sometimes identified as Arthur's illicit son) who encourages discord by revealing Lancelot's disloyalty; when Arthur pursues Lancelot into France, Modred seizes the throne and creates a civil war; he is killed by Arthur at the Battle of Camlann.

Morgan le Fay   Arthur's half-sister; as a witch and enchantress, she creates various disturbances at Camelot.

Nennius   Welsh monk whose *The History of the Britons*, written in about 800, is the earliest surviving work to mention Arthur's defeat of the Anglo-Saxons at Mount Badon.

Perceval   a knight of the Round Table who is a leading seeker of the Grail.

Round Table   first mentioned by Robert Wace in his 1155 *Roman de Brut*; it is generally assumed to signify the equality of the knights, for no knight has to sit higher or lower than any other.

Tintagel Castle   castle in southwest England where Arthur was presumably conceived and born, according to Geoffrey of Monmouth.

Uther Pendragon   son of Constantine and later king of Britain; Arthur's father by Ygerne.

Vortigern   a historical British chieftain of the fifth century; hired Anglo-Saxon invaders to be his soldiers and paid them with British land.

Vulgate Cycle   the set of five early thirteenth-century French stories written about Arthur by writers unknown today. One of these stories was *Prose Lancelot*, which introduces Galahad and was a major source used by Sir Thomas Malory.

Wace, Robert   author of *Roman de Brut* (1155), the first story to mention the Round Table.

Wolfram von Eschenbach   German author of *Parzival*, written about 1210, which is an important version of the story of Perceval's quest for the Holy Grail.

Ygerne   wife of duke of Cornwall but loved by Arthur's father Uther; she is seduced by Uther after Merlin makes him look like the absent duke; she is the mother of Arthur by Uther and of Morgan le Fay by her husband.

For Further Exploration

Leslie Alcock, *"By South Cadbury is that Camelot . . .":*
  The Excavation of Cadbury Castle, 1966-1970.
  London: Thames & Hudson, 1972.

Geoffrey Ashe, *King Arthur in Fact and Legend.* New
  York: Thomas Nelson, 1971.

Graeme Fife, *Arthur the King.* New York: Sterling,
  1991.

Elizabeth Jenkins, *The Mystery of King Arthur.* New
  York: Dorset, 1990.

Norris J. Lacy, ed., *The Arthurian Encyclopedia.* New
  York: Garland, 1986.

John Matthew, ed., *An Arthurian Reader: Selections
  from Arthurian Legend, Scholarship, and Story.*
  Wellingborough, England: Aquarian Press, 1988.

Works Consulted

Leslie Alcock, *Arthur's Britain: History and Archaeology.* New York: St. Martin's Press, 1971.

Geoffrey Ashe, *Avalonian Quest.* London: Methuen, 1982.

Geoffrey Ashe, *King Arthur's Avalon.* New York: Dutton, 1958.

Richard Barber, *The Figure of Arthur.* Totowa, NJ: Roman Littlefield, 1972.

Arthur C. L. Brown, *The Origin of the Grail Legend.* New York: Russell & Russell, 1966.

Mary Caine, *The Glastonbury Zodiac.* Torquay, England: Grael Communications, 1978.

Richard Cavendish, *King Arthur and the Grail.* New York: Taplinger, 1978.

Roger Sherman Loomis, *The Development of Arthurian Romance.* London: Hutchinson University Library, 1963.

Karen Maltwood, *A Guide to Glastonbury's Temple of the Stars.* Cambridge, England: James Clarke, 1964. (Reissue of 1935 edition.)

Leonardo Olschki, *The Grail Castle and Its Mysteries.* Translated by J. A. Scott. Berkeley: University of California Press, 1966.

Reginald F. Treharne, *The Glastonbury Legends.* London: Cresset Press, 1967.

David A. Wilson, "The Search for the Holy Grail," *Fate,* March 1990.

Index

About the Author

Michael O'Neal was born in Elyria, Ohio, in 1949. While he was an undergraduate English major at Bowling Green State University, he developed a strong interest in books and writing. He served in the armed forces and then returned to Bowling Green to earn his doctorate. A former college teacher, O'Neal edits and writes full-time. He lives in Evergreen, Colorado, with his wife. This is his third book in the Great Mysteries series.

Picture Credits